Steele Intent

Kimberly Amato

Little Crown Media, LLC

To Oma for being my guide.
To Auntie Chris for being my teacher.
To Mutte for being my friend.
To Sheila for being my everything.

Contents

Foreword

Every human being processes things differently than another human being. Ask anyone at a car accident what happened, and you'll get different descriptions from each one of them. A description of a car can change dramatically from a gold sedan to a black truck. The directionality of the vehicles, who did what first: it's all subjective. It all depends on their history, their experience, and their faith.

There's one detail that never seems to change no matter who you talk to: they all think metal crunching in on itself is the worst sound in the world.

They're wrong.

Right after the crash, you hear moaning or other signs of life. After a few minutes, the first responders arrive on scene. Before you know it, there are dozens of people screaming commands. Police officers telling people to stand behind the safety line. Firefighters ensure the vehicles are safe to be around and aren't in danger of exploding. A different group of firefighters using the Jaws of Life to rip the metal car apart. The vehicle fighting back with squeals and grunts as the frame slowly yields to the unrelenting strength of the power tool.

Paramedics attending to the passengers inside who are precariously hanging between life and death, screaming out questions to those trapped in the mangled mess. After a few stuttering answers, they yell back to their partners: heart rates, blood pressure, injuries. I know all the words. I've heard it all before. I must have said them a million times to the captain at a crash scene.

You can hear the car's fluids pouring out of the engine onto the pavement. Sometimes it's a slow, annoying drip like a faucet. Other times, it's like a rushing stream. Sometimes, if you listen closely, you can hear the blood pumping out of a person as they scream for help.

I can hear my voice there, too, asking for information from anyone who has it. I can hear the words being told to me, but they don't ever register.

I've heard it. I've seen it. I've processed it much differently than you. I would love to hear the screeching metal. I would love to hear the screams. I wish I could hear the voices.

The worst sound in my world is the silence.

Chapter One

When I was younger, my mother used to lay on the lawn with me. Since she was a teacher, I would get long lessons about all the constellations in the night sky. Personally, I just looked up at them and made wishes. Sometimes it was for a different life; mostly it was for a dog. When I was a teenager, I would look up at them and talk to my grandparents. At my current age, it's a skill I seem to have lost.

My father told me if the sky lights up, a person in heaven bowled a strike. That's what I used to believe. Now, I just see light, an annoying light that accompanies thunder and drenching rain.

I sometimes wonder where my stars have gone. It's as if the inclement weather has bankrupted my heart of its dreams. Rain is supposed to be refreshing, a cleansing of sorts. Yet, here I stand, drenched through my clothes, leaning over a corpse trying to protect what little evidence remains, knowing full well nothing will.

As I stare at the victim's soulless eyes, I wonder what choices led her to this gruesome demise. I wonder why this young woman is lying dead and I am still breathing. What did my shrink call it? Transference. That's it. I want this woman to live and part of me wants to die.

"Detective, the bus is here," the young, blue-eyed officer yells at me. He isn't paid enough to sit here with me and get soaked, but it's the job. We all do it for reasons even we can't quantify.

Looking up the small incline, I see a black van with the unmistakable white lettering of the coroner on the side. Two men, clad in black raincoats, open the back and pull a gurney out. The body bag is somewhere on top of it, I'm sure. They begin their descent while a few other assistants slide down the side next to them. I doubt the interns signed up for late night calls in this kind of weather.

The coroner's office tries hard to keep up with the raging flood of death around us, but they inevitably fall behind. Victor tells me over and over again that insurance fraud and undocumented bodies slow him down. How can you release a body without knowing who it is or what they have? I feel bad for him. The job eats away at you. Day by day you wilt under red tape and bullshit. That's why he walks so slowly and hunched over on occasion, like now. He's exhausted.

"Jazz, you trying to be a human umbrella or just an idiot?" Victor stands next to me, holding an umbrella over my soaked body. His assistant throws a tarp over the body and surrounding area. He commands each intern to grab a corner and lift. You can hear the slight moans of disagreement as they do it. The bright blue contrasts with the watered-down red on the ground as water begins to pool on it, weighing it down.

"Ever the delicate flower I see, Victor. I was trying to protect what little evidence I could." My tone is one hundred percent sarcastic. I've always been this way, and I doubt it will ever change. I guess it's one of my biggest flaws. It's a knee-jerk response, easier to deliver in a pinch. Victor's known this for years; my friends accept it as part of my charm or lack thereof.

"Considering you look like you entered a wet T-shirt contest, I'll take it there's little to none left." He motions to my white, soaked-to-the-bone shirt. "You might have wanted to wear a lighter-colored bra." Looking down at my chest, I see my black bra shows easily through my shirt. It was clean, and it was available when I got the call. In reality, I doubt anyone would have noticed the difference.

"Just do what you can. Okay, Victor?" I push him gently on the right shoulder. Even sarcasm fails me sometimes since I have nothing witty to shoot back at him.

He squats down next to the body, his designer shoes sinking further into the mud. I'm sure under this police-issued plain sheet of plastic is some designer suit. Victor has never been one to shy away from expensive looks or cologne. He's one of those slender men who are solid muscle, but not overly built. His dark hair is always cut very short. The lone diamonds in his ears seem brighter against his dark skin. He sometimes complains about his credit cards being on life support, but then goes out and gets something new and shiny. Who am I to nitpick? He pays his bills on time and still manages to put some away for his retirement. In this field, you have to find something to blow off steam. He could be a gambler, alcoholic, or an abusive husband. He's just a metrosexual.

It's during scenes like this that I'm thankful for his cologne addiction. In the office, you could smell him from a mile away. His office is probably the best smelling morgue in the tristate area. Right now, though, all I smell is some high-priced, manly smell. I'll take that over a decomposing body and an area that smells like a garbage dump threw up.

"Looks similar to the vic a few weeks ago. That's all I can give you right now." He glances at the time. "You're going to be late." Victor's voice pulls me out of my reverie.

I glance down at my watch. It has so much water in it the numbers look like I took too much acid. I know Victor's going to mention he told me to buy a more dependable waterproof watch. Not just for days like these, but considering I always leave my watch on in the shower, it was a smart suggestion. Just too expensive for my taste.

I wish I didn't have to ask. "What time is it?"

He smiles up at me; he's saying I told you so without ever actually saying it.

"Almost four," Victor says as he turns his attention back to the task at hand.

"Fuck." I am so late; crap, I'm always late.

"You, bottom right, will you hold up the damn tarp? It's not rocket science. You hold a piece of plastic up above your pretty little head," Victor screams at the intern. "Where the hell did these new kids come from? I swear the pool of educated interns get dumber every year," he mumbles to himself.

Victor never did have patience for stupidity. Looking down at my body, I get the full picture all at once. My clothes are soaked, I'm late, and there's a dead woman at my feet. This day gets better with every waking minute. At moments like this, sleep and hiding under the covers is just what the doctor would order. Sadly, adults have to do things that we wish we could avoid daily.

"You've got fresh clothes in the trunk," Victor replies to my inner monologue. It's like he can reach into my mind just by seeing my expressions, which is very creepy sometimes. "Before you ask, we made sure your backup case always has a change of clothes. I'll try to be nicer to my interns while you're gone, but I can't promise anything."

"Why?" I feel very small asking that question. Victor must hear it in my voice.

"Hadley, Frankie, and I try to keep you on your game. If you're asking why I can't be nicer to the interns, blame the education system," he says as he waves me away.

Walking backwards, stepping through more puddles, I sarcastically reply, "Ah yes, what superheroine needs one sidekick when she can have three. Have you all decided on capes or just the tight leather?"

"Neither. Our wonderful main heroine is too damn cheap to buy us a drink. let alone leather. Now get out of here before I send my interns to help you dress. Trust me, they'd be more useful to you than me," he says with some finality as he turns his attention back to the body on the ground. He slides his palm over his face as his assistant struggles with the body bag.

It's times like these where I could kiss him as a thank-you. I never think twice about my cases in the trunk. One has always contained various items needed for a crime scene—caution tape, flares, normal stuff. I never knew what the other contained, and I never actually took the time to figure it out. Leave it to my friends to make sure I'm taken care of, even when I don't do it myself.

Smiling at the thought, I remember I have someplace to be and run up the sloppy mud pile of an incline. It's the one place in the world I wish I was never late to but religiously am. I wouldn't change it for anything in the world. Regardless of my horrible time management skills, the location is what my heart needs to beat right now.

Running through various puddles and mud pits, I can feel the water slosh in my boots. In the back of my mind, I know I'm going to have to dry them out. Hopefully, they'll still fit after all this. Knowing the case is in the trunk and I have leather seats, I fumble in my pockets for my keys to open the lift gate. The same beaded chain that I've had for years stares up at me from the palm of my hand: my name, Jasmine, in all pink, purple, and other girly-colored beads. The only material gift I ever received from my older brother. Too bad it's on a rather manly set of keys. Hitting the unlock buttons more than once, the trunk starts to open on its own.

The one thing I realized during my college years of fooling around in the back of a truck is that tall people need headroom. I know gas prices are on the rise and everyone wants to ditch the guzzling climate-killer SUVs, but I still own one. It's the only way I can manage to change in the back without slamming myself unconscious on the ceiling. These new smaller cars are made for short, thin people who carry nothing more than a pen or a pair of sunglasses. As a member of the force, you have to carry a shit ton of gear with you. Don't even get me started on if you have kids. People do require things to travel with them.

Like jeans that stick to your flesh when you desperately need to get out of them, a small car like a Prius just doesn't cut it. My hand smashes the back-corner panel window as my pants finally break free. The throbbing in my wrist annoys me as I frantically slide into the dry outfit from my kit. Grabbing my soaked boots, I slide over the back seat and sit down. After struggling to get them back on, I climb into the front and start the engine. Various lights flash across the dash before they disappear. Pulling my seatbelt on, I pull away from the crime scene and onto the roadway.

I fly through traffic, police lights flashing as I cross various intersections. The wiper blades slosh the water back and forth. The visibility is minimal at best. Using the lights might be totally illegal, but some lines can be blurred when the greater good is involved. My dad taught me that. Of course, my father also taught me that Woodstock was just a wonderful place for music and some fun. It wasn't until my brother and I found his picture in the centerfold of the anthology of the book that he admitted he was there. We would joke then about him smoking weed there. His comment, "It was the sixties." Like that made it all right. It's times like these when I miss him: when my wiper blades sweep across the glass with a beat that sounds like a folk song he used to sing; when I think about never getting to comment on his rolling skills; when I think we were never able to argue about music and his bluegrass roots. He always told me to be leery of authority. Here I am, the authority, breaking the rules I swore to uphold. Irony must love me.

Pulling into the parking lot, aimlessly looking for a space that isn't a lake or taken is not an easy task. Once again, I choose to bend another rule and pull up in a fire zone, grabbing the police parking badge and shoving it on the dashboard for all to see. My shoes are still wet, the rain continues to drench the earth beneath it, and my hair is a mess. Yet, like every good superheroine, I must attend to my duties.

Tearing out of my car faster than a speeding bullet, I dodge rain droplets, jump over puddles of muddy water, and manage to get to the steps before I slip. Landing on my right knee against the staircase instantly sends pain searing into the joint. Climbing the steps, I enter the one place I dreaded from the time I could walk. School.

The sound of my shoes sloshing and squeaking echoes through the empty halls, signaling a late parent. Every step announces my presence as I desperately want to remain quiet. Teachers peer through their open doors as I pass. I swear some of them sneer at me, marking me in their memory as *that parent*. It's like walking to the principal's office, and even at my age it makes the hair on the back of my neck stand up. Room 104, door closed. Shit.

I knock gently on the door before opening it and stepping inside. My heart instantly drops. Chase sits quietly with his wrestling action figures. Alone. I left him alone, again. His teacher, an older woman with slightly graying hair, sits at her desk. Glasses rest at the end of her nose as she grades her papers quietly. If I didn't know any better, I would say she was the stereotypical old lady teacher. Then again, who am I to complain about her looks. If not for the hair dye in my bathroom, I'd probably look older than I am. Neither of them notices me, so I knock again.

"Mrs. Steele?" Her harsh tone matches her expression. She leans back and slides the glasses off her face. They hang loosely on a chain as she looks me up and down.

If she knew what I was dealing with, I'm sure she would give me a bit of a break. I wish I could tell her where I just was and let her know I'm not a bad guardian. I'm sure she would say we're both in the same boat. We both work hard to protect future generations from a life in crime or subpar living. Her tone, though, still irks me.

"Doctor Steele," I say ruder than I mean to. The whole humility thing is a work in progress, I swear. I extend my hand out to her, but she just looks at it. I've already met her a few times this year, so this tit for tat is hardly necessary. Adults and our egos.

"Yes, well, Doctor Steele, we are not a daycare. Regardless of the fact that Chase is an exceptional student, I cannot babysit him. I've given you leeway during the adjustment period, but it's been long enough. Don't you think?" She stands at her desk, staring at me and my hand hanging in midair.

I lower my forgotten limb and shove my hand in my pocket. I feel my disdain rising and know I'm likely to snap. I know teachers don't have it easy. Their jobs can be more difficult than mine at times. The dead don't answer me back like her students do, but I'm not in the right frame of mind at the moment. It takes everything in my power to control my emotions and not lash out physically at this woman.

"I'm sorry, I didn't catch your name," I say, trying to be polite. Truthfully, at this moment in time, her name eludes me. I want to sit her down and show her images of brutal crime scenes and other vile things to get her to back off. It's a defense mechanism of sorts as she continues to size me up. One thing I've learned never to do—walk away from a fight. But I don't want to make the rest of the school year miserable for Chase, so I have to play it safe.

"It's on the syllabus for the school year, and we've met more than once. I can assume you haven't actually read the documentation I sent home?" I watch her shift her stance. Her arms fold in front of her, and she leans on her back-right leg. Everything about her posture screams defensiveness. It's as if she's taunting me to play a game that I always win. She's not aware of this, of course, but if she wants to play, I'm in.

"Sadly, I haven't. Much too busy filling out police reports to prevent low-life cretins from entering your school before helping Chase with his homework. So, if you wish for those unsightly individuals to enter the establishment, I will gladly let them. Then I would be able to enjoy more free time with my nephew rather than be late to pick him up," I finish in a huff. I swear I sounded like my mother. I shiver at the thought.

"Margaret Johnson," she says calmly. Her entire demeanor softens, her stance more level as her arms rest loosely at her sides.

"Thank you. I'm sure you know, but I'm Jasmine Steele." I meet her gaze and she simply nods in agreement. Her attention turns to Chase, who's probably been watching the interaction like a hawk. He says I embarrass him too much when it comes to things like this, so he probably wants to crawl under a rock right now.

"Chase tells me you're a homicide detective. He never mentioned you being a doctor as well," she says, but her attention never leaves my nephew.

"Chase is a good kid, never lies."

She immediately turns her attention back to me. Her forehead wrinkles in confusion as her eyes search mine for some sort of answers. It's interesting for someone like me to see. Watching all those emotions play out on a human being's face is very telling. Imagine a movie where the villain tells the victim all the reasons why he's doing everything before he kills the guy. It's like that.

"I'm a psychotherapist. Doctor sounds a bit better when you're trying to trump someone," I say sheepishly.

The wrinkles disappear from her forehead but migrate to the corners of her mouth as her lips curl into a smirk. The altercation seems behind us now. I wonder if it was really necessary to begin with, but like I said before, adults and our egos. I know being late is very wrong and this woman has a life outside of work as well, but death waits for no one. The crime scene is a priority so that bad people go away for good. I just want to wish away everything right now, but the clouds are blocking the stars. I doubt I would know how to make a wish anyway. Never worked before.

I turn my attention to my nephew, sitting quietly during this whole interaction. His head rests in his hands, feet swinging under the chair as he waits patiently for me to get my foot out of my ass. He's so young in age but more of an adult than I am. I wish he could just enjoy being a kid, but life happens when you least expect it.

"Chase, you ready to go?" I ask.

He says nothing as he slides out of the metal containment unit they call a desk. He pulls on his jacket and prepares for the inclement weather outside. It's methodical, precise—just like his father used to do it. Then, the backpack, right strap before left. Always the same. His action figures push against the sides of his bag, but they won't break free. He stops in front of me but says nothing. Margaret nods to me before Chase and I leave the classroom.

His head hangs low as he walks, as if he's counting the tiles on the floor. I don't know what I could say or do to make it better. He's got all the toys any boy his age could want. Frankly, my small house can't handle any more. Chase's quick pace gets him to the front door, where the rain has miraculously stopped.

He silently gets into the back seat and buckles himself in. No fuss, no need for help, nothing. Just that unbearable silence again. Leaving the lights off and trying to be a good example for the kid, I pull out onto the road. The rain suddenly unleashes its fury again as if to warn me of an impending conversation I don't want to have. The sky lights up with purplish-blue bolts of electricity illuminating the world around me.

"You were late again, so I did my homework in school." His voice is so soft I can barely make out what he says.

The thunder rolls across the streets, slamming into my ears ferociously.

"Yeah, honey, I'm sorry." He nods his head weakly and leans to the side. I try to watch him in my rearview mirror, but he's hiding in the blind spot.

The sky lights up again in another burst of fractured light.

"Ten, eleven, twelve, thirteen . . ." The sky erupts again, more powerful this time.

"The storms not that far away," he finishes.

He leans back into an area I can see him, a smile spread across his face.

"Where'd you learn that?" I ask.

He looks at me in the rearview mirror, and his hazel eyes fill with sadness as he sinks into his seat. Whatever joy was just there is gone.

"In one of Daddy's notebooks," he says.

Shit. If there are topics of conversation not to discuss, besides my escapades in college, the death of my brother and his wife are number one on my list. Sometimes it was unavoidable; other times I felt as if I walked into a steaming pile of shit. This was a steaming pile moment.

"That's great," I mumble to myself. Maybe if I avoid the very large elephant in the car, it will just turn into a small arachnid. It can be that annoying spider in the car that never shows itself, but you see webs on your windshield. That would work for me.

"Why were you late?" He plays with his fingers, nervous. His father did that when we were growing up. I remember he would fidget like that when he had to talk to our parents about something. Most times he would mumble it out in a horribly jammed up sentence, and my parents had to decipher it. I understand that now. I have learned how to understand Chase's mumbles, and it's a new language.

"Work," I answer.

"Bad day?" He pushes slightly.

"Yep," I add, trying to calm the conversation. This isn't territory I want to tread in at the moment.

"How old?" he prods again.

"How old is who?" Deflection is my strong suit, I think.

"The dead person," he finishes.

There is one thing I can say for certain: slamming on brakes in rain is not conducive to stopping. Hydroplaning across a lane of traffic is not fun. I repeat, not an activity I wish to do again. My SUV slides to a stop at a red light, and I slowly release the death grip I have on the steering wheel. I turn around and look at Chase sitting calmly behind my seat.

"What makes you think there was a dead person?" I ask pointedly.

"I wasn't sure until you freaked out. Please don't do that again. Papa Jon said running through red lights is bad." I laugh at his reference to my father—the one man I idolized as a child for being strong, intelligent, someone to depend on, everything a man should be. He also killed a forest with all the red-light tickets he was mailed in his lifetime.

"Yes, he also told me there was once a president named Wilbert Homie." My mouth breaks into a smile before I can reel it in; my father had good moments.

"I know. Daddy told me he used to sleep through study times."

I feel the smile slide off my face. Turning back around in my seat, I watch the windshield wipers cross the glass, cleaning off the excess fluids. It's funny how I hide from memories of my father. Chase remembers him fondly, and that's good. Buried within the hurt of being forgotten, the tears of being ignored, the disappointment after years of knowing he will never respect me, there are happy times. The problem is those times are so few and far between.

"Buddy, why don't we go home, okay? We'll talk more there."

Chase goes back to staring out the window. I go back to thinking about how I can't be a parent. I'm not good at it. I'm not ready for it, and frankly I never asked for it. I just wanted to be the fun aunt who came over to play. The one every kid on the block wanted to hang out with. In the end, I wanted to be able to drop the kids off at home on a massive sugar high.

Pulling up in the driveway outside my house, I realize something and it drowns me. I brought the kid home. He's my kid. He's my responsibility and my job to guide him through life. It's been a year since I've been his guardian, and today it hits me like a ton of bricks. Maybe it's because of the dead girl, but I doubt it. I've seen plenty of bodies since I buried Chase's family, buried my only brother. No, today's different, and I need to focus on something else.

I'm a complete robot when I walk inside the house, mechanically removing my coat, hanging it up, and placing the keys on a small hook. Chase does the same with his coat before we both remove our shoes. He struggles with one of the laces, and I kneel down to untie it. One day this kid is going to be an adult and not need me anymore. I'll be truly alone then.

He rushes into the kitchen, grabs his cup, and fills it with milk. One thing's for sure: our evening tradition will never be denied regardless of the day's events. I grab a tall glass, fill it with milk, then get the chocolate syrup and two spoons before sitting across from him.

"So, what's up?" I sound like a five-year-old talking to his mother. I hate when my voice betrays me.

"Stuff." He rolls the cup around on its edge, one full complete rotation. Mom did that a lot; she said it helped her to focus when she was thinking.

"Like what? Wrestling matches? Pokémon? Those silly pens with the funny hair? Girls?" Hopefully I covered all the things he's into at this point in time.

"Eww. Girls are annoying, and they don't like wrestling." He lets go of the cup and his eyes meet mine. They're gray today. The color changing eyes are a recessive gene in my family and we both share it. Most people can hide their emotions with a poker face or a stoic expression of some kind. Chase and I wear it in our eyeballs. When they're gray, something is really wrong. Stress, fear, whatever it is—gray is not a good color.

"While I understand girls not liking wrestling, what's really on your mind?" Chase opens his mouth to speak, and I know a diversion tactic is coming. "Before you say it, I only like the choreographed sport because you do. Trust me, I would rather watch a *Barney* marathon than sit through another fake ladders and chairs match." I hand him the chocolate syrup.

Chase promptly closes his mouth. He turns his attention to making his chocolate milk. I know he needs a moment to think.

"I couldn't see today." His voice is weak, shallow.

"Couldn't see what?" I look over at him, but his eyes never leave the concoction in front of him. "The blackboard? Maybe we should get your eyes checked. Everyone in the family has had glasses, contacts, or surgery, so it wouldn't hurt. Hell, maybe you need those special gamer glasses. They're pretty cool."

"No. I couldn't see the sky." He stops spinning the spoon and slinks lower into his chair. If he could be one with the floor, he would be.

"It was raining, sweetie. Tomorrow it should be clear," I say, not quite understanding the reference.

"So, I'll see heaven tomorrow then?" He smiles ever so slightly.

"What do you mean see heaven?"

"You said Daddy and Mommy are in heaven with Papa and Grandma."

"Yeah, they are." I hope.

"I couldn't see them today. It was cloudy. I usually look up at lunch to make sure they're up there. Once I feel one of them watching me, I know it's okay to play."

"Why wouldn't it be okay to play?"

"Because I'm having fun without them."

And there it is.

Chase gets up, stands next to me, leaving his chocolate milk behind. I see the tears in his eyes that want to fall but he holds them in. Eventually he'll talk to me, but for now I let him be. He just hugs me very tightly.

"I love you, Aunt Jazz." His voice is nothing more than a whisper.

I want to pull him tight and make the world right for him. I'm not sure I'm in a good place to do that, let alone know how. I simply hold onto him as long as he allows me. He steps out of the embrace, turns around, and goes to his room. I hear the door click shut, and I stare at his forgotten drink. He's never gone to bed without at least a sip or two. Our tradition is broken.

Aunt Jazzie, pick up phone!

My cell phone blares in my pocket. I used to love Chase yelling at me as my ringtone back in the day. Chase was three when he recorded it. I was still an aspiring writer, and this silly tone reminded me why I was working so hard. I managed to write one novel with the full intention of finishing the series, but life got in the way. The killer was never found, the victims never vindicated, and the series remains unfinished. Who knows if people even cared about it; sales were horrible.

My screenplays were never finished. I still have the files on my computer I can't bring myself to delete. If they could collect dust, I'd have a dust mite infestation. Either way, he's seven now, and all I write now are police reports. I should change this ringtone to something more professional, like a metal song or something. Anything to freak out the criminals I deal with on a daily basis, or maybe some of my co-workers. For some reason though, I can't bring myself to change the ringtone. Another thing I can't let go of—Chase's innocence.

"Steele," I say, my voice professional even though I have a milk mustache.

"Did you make it?" It must be check-in time. Frankie rarely calls me when she's alone, so Hadley must be with her. I don't think she trusts what our conversations might turn into if it was just the two of us. The gentle sound of another extension being clicked confirms my suspicion.

"Yes. Hi, Hadley."

"How'd you know I was here?" Her cheerful voice radiates through the phone.

"Because Frankie is nothing without a side order of her roommate Hadley to annoy. Not to mention in today's age of modern technology, picking up another extension is a dying art."

"Yeah, well . . ." Hadley starts but never finishes. I hear some odd static before the sound pretty much dies out. Their muffled voices hit my ear, but I can't decipher any of it. I hear one line click again before the softest voice comes through.

"You sure you're okay? Victor mentioned you being . . . off," she says.

"Frankie, I'm fine. Just tired," I lie. It's what I do lately. Lie to the kid. Lie to myself. Lies, lies, and more lies. I spout them out so easily now I don't know where they begin and the truth ends or vice versa.

"I know you better than that. You want to talk about it?" she pushes gently. If there is anyone who can get me to talk, it's her.

"Don't try to analyze me, Frankie. The department pays for a shrink I don't know to pick my brain." That came out of my mouth harsher than I meant. I hear Hadley in the background arguing something, then that familiar clicking sound.

"She's just trying to help you out, sour puss." I can see Hadley's face scrunching up as she speaks. She's an animated actress who somehow manages to bring home a constant paycheck and not be in debt. Go figure.

"She ate Fruit Loops again, didn't she?" I can hear Frankie laughing. Like Chase's laugh, it is one of the things that allows my heart to still beat.

"I have a commercial audition tomorrow. I have to be upbeat and perky. Fruit Loops are the cereal of hyper children everywhere. I thought I'd give it a try," Hadley says as she crunches away at more chemically created cereal.

"Well, scale it back a bit. Just a loop or two," I say, drinking my chocolate milk.

"Funny, Jazz, really funny," Hadley says through a mouthful of food.

"In all seriousness, Jazz, what's going on with this new body of yours?" Frankie interjects.

"News travels fast," I answer.

"Like I said, we talked to Victor earlier, and he said the girl was in pretty bad shape," Frankie says, her voice more serious than before.

"Let's just say this isn't a part Hadley would want to play in a film," I answer.

"Why? Most of her films involve her screaming in her nightgown as she runs away from a serial killer," Frankie says. She knows when to stop pushing against the walls I have up. Like my nephew, I'll talk when I'm ready. Not to mention, Frankie should have the case file on her desk sometime soon. We'll need some kind of criminal profile for us to go on.

I do miss this constant banter between all of us. I wish we had more time to do it, but careers and life have gotten in the way.

"Jazz, come on. Tell us," Hadley pushes, the sugar rush getting the better of her.

"Wish I knew more. She's the second young girl I've seen this week. Don't know much else." Another lie. My gut tells me there is so much more to it, but I can't deal with theories or hypotheticals right now. I need facts, supported by science and my rationale.

"Don't forget beaten to a pulp," Hadley adds.

"And strangled," Frankie says.

"Apparently you two know more than I do," I retort.

"Victor," they say in unison on the other end of the phone.

"Look, I'm pretty tired. Frankie, if you want to take a crack at the profile, I'll hook you up with the files. I'm too tired to do it myself, and I don't trust anyone else. Hadley, stay out of trouble and try to get a role that doesn't involve you dying. I can't handle that either."

"Okay, I'll talk to you later." The phone clicks off.

Silence engulfs the conversation as I listen to Frankie breathing.

"Jasmine," she says softly.

"Yeah, Frankie?"

"I'm here."

There she goes always saying the right thing at the right time. We went to graduate school together, and I thought we would never get through it all. Two Madonna concerts later, and we helped each other graduate early. Then, she had to go show me up and get her doctorate before me. Oh wait, that's still on my to-do list. The same list that keeps growing by the day, and I don't even know where to start to even attempt to shrink it down.

"Thanks." My voice wavers betraying me.

"Love and hugs from the nuthouse," she says with a slight chuckle.

Before I can reply, the phone line dies. The nuthouse—that just makes me laugh. They were a nuthouse all right, but I was a willing participant in the insanity to keep my sanity. Go figure. I think irony is not just laughing at me, but planning a ball in my honor. The ironic part, though, is I'm not invited.

I need sleep. To dream. I think I subconsciously prevent myself from sleeping. I toss and turn, stare at the clock, play a game on my antiquated handheld, and try to sleep later. I can hear Chase doing the same thing, but with his game system. The sound of his Pokémon trainer heading into battle is crystal clear through the thin walls. Have I mentioned how much I really dislike Pokémon? It's like Barney, but instead of being purple, it's a yellow thing that sounds way too damn chipper.

Oh, how my life has changed. Back in the day, my bed was warm. Not just with a fancy duvet or flannel sheets, but with a living, breathing human being. I can't say for sure if life was easier then, but it was more fulfilling. I had a person I could share everything with. The ups, downs, and all those lefts and rights a cool slide has to offer. Chase's lingo is really rubbing off on me. No more game sounds coming through the wall. He must be trying to sleep.

People ask me if Chase was the reason for the mutual breakup. He wasn't. I swear on everything I hold dear in my life he had nothing to do with it. The problem was me trying to balance two new lives. I went from partner and dreamer to mother, without any remaining members of my family to assist me. I couldn't handle it, and I let the love of my life walk out. What makes it worse; she's one of my closest friends. If there is a higher power, I have to thank him for that when I see him. Note the sarcasm.

Shutting my phone off, I plug it in and place it on the end table. The door creaks open, and I glance at the clock. Eleven p.m., right on time. The sheets move, and I roll over on my back. Chase snuggles into me, and I hold him close. His nightmares have simmered down over the past year, but they still manage to disrupt his sleep patterns. I've heard him sometimes begging his father to wake up. I know what the scene looked like. I pulled my nephew out of the car and saw my brother's eyes stare at me. Empty.

I feel the tears form in my eyes, and I blink them away. Chase doesn't need more of this. He needs to be held so he can sleep. I take several deep breaths to calm my emotions. I feel his body get heavier as his breathing shifts. His arms fall limp; his left leg twitches a bit so I know he's out. He must have been really tired. Normally it takes a lot longer for him to pass out.

My arms secure Chase next to me, and finally I feel safe enough to close my eyes. Maybe tonight I will dream about what could have been, or maybe I will just relax enough to rest. I don't mind either one. I just don't want to think right now.

Close eyes, lean head back . . . rest.

Chapter Two

Beeping. Incessant beeping. The alarm blaring at me like a five-alarm fire. I have to stop staying up so late at night. Mother told me if I just lay in bed, I'd feel rested in the morning. I swear she was just saying that to get me to go lie down. I wonder if I say little white lies to Chase in order to get him to listen to me. I might sound like my mom, but I doubt I'm anything like her. She was amazing, and I'm just me.

There's only one smell that could wake me up after such a horrible night's rest: coffee. The fact that it's brewing means another adult is around. I pop up quickly, my eyes darting wildly around the room, adjusting to the light. My left hand pats around on the end table looking for my glasses. Once found, my hand wraps around them before slamming them on my face, The finger smudges blinding me worse than my actual vision issues. Quickly rubbing them clean, I replace them and enjoy the ability to see clearly.

Another noise in the kitchen pulls my attention back. Standing up, I walk to the bedroom door and grab the baseball bat hiding behind it. Slowly, as to not make a sound, I walk down the hall with the bat ready to strike.

"Aunt Jazz, I can hear you." Of course, the perp is a little twerp with a sense of humor. I lower the bat from its ready position and walk around the corner into the kitchen. There on the table is a steaming cup of coffee placed in front of a plate of burned toast.

"Thanks, little man. I appreciate it." I say internally high-fiving myself for remembering to just be thankful for the little things.

"It's no big deal. I was up. Besides, you snore." He says as he pulls out some sugary cereal I don't remember buying.

"I do not." I attempt to defend myself, but he's right.

"Aunt Jazz, your snoring could cause an earthquake big enough to swallow New York City."

"I doubt the whole city heard it." I smirk as I say it and grab my mug of happiness. I take a nice full swig of liquid in my mouth when I had to stop for a second. You know those moments when you aren't quite sure what's in your mouth. You want to spit it out, but you don't want to insult the person who gave it to you. Then again, you don't want to swallow because it might eat through your stomach. The kid made me coffee, so I force the hot fluid down my throat with a smile.

"Thanks, this is great!" I say with a little too much energy. He smiles and motions for me to drink up. So, I do. I chug the hot beverage as fast as I can. My mind wanders to when I made cookies for my mom as a kid. They were so badly burned you couldn't tell where the charcoal ended and cookie began.

Once I was done with the mug, I proceeded to eat the burned toast with a little bit of butter. When I wasn't looking, the little rascal filled my mug back up. I added as much milk as my twenty-ounce mug could handle, and the color stayed dark. Kid's testing me now. Has to be. Right? So, I drink it all again, as fast as possible. Then, I devour the rest of the bread to hopefully absorb whatever acid I just shoved down there. Chase places a bottle of water next to me, and I proceed to chug that as well. The coffee was a bit hotter than I like, and I need to wash that flavor out of my mouth.

"You really drank it." He asks dumbfounded.

"Of course I did. You made it for me." I sputter between chugs of water.

"I put nine scoops of coffee in the maker." He sits back and folds his arms.

My stomach lurches at the thought. Just smile and say something witty. Maybe the kid won't see through it.

"I didn't notice." My sad attempt falls flat.

"Yes, you did." He smiles back at me.

I stare blankly at him, but he knows the real score. This kid was truly testing me, and I fell for it. I did what any parent would do, and now he knows. This is why there's nine months when you're pregnant, to get your shit in order. Not what I got. For me, it was bam, here's a kid. Now go raise him. No manuals or months to mentally prepare. Truthfully, I don't know if it would help.

"I'm supposed to put three scoops in." He cuts off my train of thought as he gets up from his chair. He grabs the pot, pours the remaining coffee down the drain and cleans the container. The way he moves around the kitchen setting everything up for a fresh pot of coffee makes me smile. It's really nice that he's doing this for me, but it also shows he's becoming a bit more comfortable in his home.

"Thank you." He pushes the on button and hugs my leg. After maybe a second, he pulls away and walks down the hall. I am so confused.

"Stop thinking too much, Aunt Jazz. I don't want to be late for school."

Did I mention to you he was a smart-ass? I grab my travel coffee mug and pour as much normal java as I can in there. I put some milk in it, and I see the lighter shade of brown staring back at me. Perfect. Maybe that beeping was a blessing in disguise.

"Aunt Jazz, I smell smoke. You're still thinking too much." He's laughing again.

"Ha, ha, funny little man. Get your stuff ready."

Walking to my bedroom, I hear him saying good morning to his fish. He has a few neon tetra fish swimming aimlessly in a medium-size fish tank. He named them after all our dead family members, plus one named Bubba. I don't know why that name came into play, but they help keep him calmer. Sometimes he'll talk to them about varying things from school to whatever is on the television. He does all the work to clean them too, which was a massive shock and a half for me.

The weather is brighter today after the full day of stormy skies. My car looks shiny and new thanks to the natural car wash. I can't be bothered to do it myself with the little free time I have. Stepping outside, I take a deep breath and feel a slight chill as the cold air seeps into my lungs. Chase darts under my arms and rushes to the car. Another day, another dollar, I guess.

This early in the morning I prefer to avoid the silence that once again permeates the car. If I had a migraine, sure, but after drinking pure adrenaline in the form of sludge, I need something to do. My shaky hand turns on the radio to the satellite station playing eighties music all the time. Something about that decade always makes me smile. Simple music, songs that are easy to remember, and nothing in your face like music is right now. I couldn't tell you half of the song titles, let alone any of the band names, but I can mumble along the lyrics with the best of them.

"Those aren't the right words," my nephew pipes up from the back seat.

"Say what?" I ask.

He doubles down. "You're singing the wrong words."

"How would you know? You weren't even a thought in your father's eye when this song came out," I answer him quickly.

"At every live wrestling event, this is Conroy Jameson's entrance song. They play it all the time, especially when he won the title against J. G. Holms," Chase says, referring to the matches I always suffer through. I don't get this fake crap, but he enjoys it. Personally, I think he enjoys jumping on me from the top of the couch, but whatever.

"What are the actual words, masterful one?" I ask with a slight hint of playful sarcasm in my tone. Let's see how good his musical prowess is.

"Why should I do the work for you? You always tell me if you want to learn something, you have to look it up. When you get to work, go to Google and look up the lyrics for Skid Row's 'Youth Gone Wild,'" he says with a serious look on his face. The kid just schooled me in the worst possible way.

"You just think you're smarter than me kiddo," I answer with a slight laugh.

"Sometimes. I can't drive, so you win that battle." He smiles brightly at me in the rearview mirror.

"I see. I'm a glorified chauffeur? Driving Mr. Chase?" I say in a horrible British accent that forces a deep belly laugh to erupt from within me.

"I don't know what that means." He stares blankly at me. "But you do have really cool hair."

"Excuse me? I'm going gray, little man; I don't know what's so cool about that," I answer..

"You have hair. It gives me hope. In all the pictures you have of Daddy, he's bald. I don't want to be that way when I grow up," he says honestly.

"Well, the balding gene does run in our family, sweetheart. My daddy was bald, too; he just never admitted it to himself."

"Yeah, Papa and Daddy liked ripped jeans."

"Not jeans, like the ones you wear. G-e-n-e," I spell out for him. "It's something that . . . well, when you are conceived . . . growing in your mama's belly . . ." I stumble over my words as I realize the conversation that I'm having with my nephew is not ideal. Glancing in the mirror, I can tell by the expression on his face he's waiting for me to continue my train of thought. My stomach flips. My hands begin to sweat.

"Aunt Jazz?"

"You know what? You should ask your teacher about genes and what they do. She'd be able to tell you more than I ever could. I was never really good at science," I say quickly.

"What's conceived mean?" He follows up with a question that makes my heart pound in my chest like a wild hyena.

"Wow, look at that, we're here!" I say, pulling up to the curb outside his school. "Have a great day learning, little man!"

Chase unbuckles his seat belt, picks up his backpack, and kisses me on the cheek twice. I asked him about it once. He said one was for being his aunt and one was for taking care of him. Grounds me more than anything else right now. I watch as he hops out of the car to walk up to the front doors. A few other boys find him and Chase's hands begin their animated waving around. He talks just like his father, all hands when he's excited.

"What the hell is the matter with you, Jasmine? You don't mention the word conceive to a seven-year-old! Especially when it involves your brother and things he did that you don't ever want to think about." I rub my eyes frantically, trying to get the image out of my head. Mental note to myself: thinking of your older brother's sex life is not something any little sister should do. Let alone after drinking pure acid and only having two pathetic pieces of burned toast to absorb it. It's almost as bad as thinking about how I got here. Nope!

Aunt Jazzie, pick up phone!

Thankfully, my cell phone pulls my attention away before my thoughts hit the point of no return. Digging through my bag next to me, I search for my phone.

Aunt Jazzie, pick up phone!

"I heard you the first time, Chase. I'm trying to find the fucking thing." The damn thing taunts me as I search for it. Glancing up at my reflection, I notice the Bluetooth earpiece and settle into my seat. I seriously think I'm losing my marbles. Clicking the button on the device, I connect to the call.

"Steele." It's then that I look down and see my offending cell phone hiding in the door pocket by my legs. How it got there, I'll never know. If it had teeth, I'd be missing a foot by now.

"Hello?"

No one speaks.

"Hello," I say into the microphone again. I hate all these prank calls. I get about five or a six a day now, and it's rather frustrating.

"Okay, great, thanks for letting me know that solar energy could be a better way to go. Please lose my number and fuck—"

"In the end, everyone is the same. We all turn to dust." The soft-spoken voice cuts me off.

I laugh slightly in response.

"You practicing your dialogue, Had? Good delivery, but it sounds like every other horror film out there."

"Don't think you're untouchable." The tone changes pitch, harsher, more direct. "You and your son."

My heart pounds viciously in my chest, forcing me to slow my breathing. I open my mouth to reply, but nothing comes out. I hear the telltale signs of a disconnected call beeping in my ear. I flip through the call log and go to dial the last incoming number. Private listing. I quickly dial Hadley.

"What's up, home slice?" she answers in her usual perky voice. I'd normally have a funny response for her, but not today.

"You didn't just call me, did you? And you're thirty-two, so stop trying to sound like you're twenty-one." I try to keep my voice even and not sound as frantic as I feel. It's one thing my family instilled in me since birth. You should always sound normal, even when you're going out of your mind. Never air your dirty laundry for the world to see or hear about. It's one of those things we question later because in the end, family are the ones that hurt you more than anyone else.

"At least I still look like I'm young, unlike miss I-have-to-dye-my-hair-once-a-month-to-cover-up-the-gray, and no, I didn't call you. Why?" she replies, her voice sounding slightly concerned.

"No reason. Just checking. When's your audition?" My voice cracks a bit. She knows I'd never call before an audition to wish her luck. She always gets a call from me after it, so I don't give her any bad juju.

"In about an hour." The nerves start to show in her voice. I've heard it before, and I know she's started to pick up on my charade.

"Good luck." I hear a sharp intake of air on the other end of the line.

"You so did NOT say that."

"What?" I ask quickly, my mind focusing on other things right now.

"You never say good luck. That gives bad luck. It's break a leg," she says defiantly.

"Okay, then break both." My voice must sound uncaring and almost cruel, but I need to get her off the phone to make another call.

"Too late. I'm already jinxed," she says.

"Whatever you say, Hadley. I need to run."

I can hear her inhale before I quickly disconnect the call. I'm sure I'll get a call later telling me how her success or lack thereof today was my fault. I can't handle that right now. I quickly dial Victor at work. As the phone rings in my ear, I pull out into traffic and head to the office as quickly as I legally can.

"To what do I owe the pleasure?" His usual greeting calms me a bit, allowing me to gain control over my heartbeat.

"Do you know anyone with a private line?" I ask quickly.

"Only about half of the known world. Why?"

"Let me rephrase that: Does anyone you know with a private line have my number?"

"That's an awfully vague question, don't you think? There are any number of people who could look up your number and create a private one for themselves. Jasmine, it's really easy to find you and to make a number private. You're going to have to narrow down your question." He answers with more information than needed, but I understand why.

"I just received a very weird phone call, and it's freaking me out a little bit," I say honestly for the first time today. Maybe he can help me sort this out in my head before I get to work.

"What did they say?" he asks, and I can hear some of his tools touching the metal trays, the snapping a telltale sign he's removed the latex gloves from his hands.

"The voice was muffled," I blurt out before I can stop myself. I want to tell him the truth, but part of me is trying to protect those around me I love. This is not going to work in this situation.

"You got a prank call from a heavy breather?" His laughter radiates through the phone. "I wouldn't be too worried. At least you're still getting gentlemen callers, considering your proclivity for the fairer gender. Maybe I should jump to your side of the fence. Women seem rather . . . cold. Hell, I should know. I married one."

"I have no idea what I'm supposed to say to that." I have other things on my mind, and his attempt at humor is falling rather flat this morning.

"Yeah, it was a stretch, but someone had to do it. Look, don't worry too much about your secret admirer," Victor purrs through the phone. "I hate to rush, but I have patients to attend to. I'm sure you understand."

"Not like they're going anywhere, but deadlines for cases . . . got it." I disconnect the call, cutting off his laughter.

Pulling into the basement parking garage at my precinct, I hop out of the car and rush up the stairs. I stop in front of Officer Keith Garrison's desk, my hand still shaking from the call. The young man who states he has the desire and drive to be the youngest detective ever sits at his desk playing some word search game every day. He always wears this worn-out baseball cap where ever he goes. I've written him up for donning that damn cap on the job. He's got the same fucking uniform hat we all suffered through. He's no different from the rest of us, regardless of how he acts.

"Officer, can I see you in my office for a moment?" I say calmly.

He jumps at his desk and hits some buttons on the keyboard before standing abruptly. He smiles sheepishly as if caught with his hand in the cookie jar. Walking around his desk, I head down the hall to my office.

Normally, I enjoy the looks of fear on people's faces when it comes to the job. You're here to protect and serve, not to play games, be untrained, or be an asshole. Those people need not apply. Sadly, they do, and they squeak by to get a job. We're still trying to weed the bad seeds out in my home away from home. Either way, the time to deal with that is later. Right now, I need this little shit to prove to me he's capable of more than writing tickets.

I close the door and take a seat behind my desk. Garrison sits across from me, his leg bouncing frantically.

"I need to ask you something, and it cannot leave this room. Do you understand?" I say forcefully.

"Yes, ma'am," he says as he nods, almost rocking his body, in affirmation.

"If someone called me from a private number, would you be able to find out anything about the call, including the number?" I ask.

"Not the number, but I might be able to triangulate where the call originated from. That would be beyond the time frame and date the call happened. I mean those would be stored in your phone already." He nervously picks at the cuticle on his right thumb.

"If this call was answered and there was a short conversation, would you be able to access said call to record what was said?" I press, trying to sound cryptic.

"Depends if it was recorded by an intelligence agency or something similar. Sometimes phones can record these things, but it might be a slim to none chance." He continues to fidget. "May I ask why?"

I take my cell phone out of my pocket and place it in the center of my desk. I wait for him to take it, but he just stares at me blankly.

"I need you to find out everything you can about the private call I received this morning. Pull anything and get back to me as soon as possible. Okay?" I say, leaning back in my chair.

"Yes, ma'am." He grabs the phone and stands up.

"Oh, and Garrison?"

"Yes?"

"That baseball cap is not part of your uniform, is it?" I point to his head.

"No, it isn't." He lowers his gaze to the ground.

"You might want to take it off before the captain demands someone write you up again. You're a cop with a desire to move up in the ranks, right? So, don't go blowing it by having your jacket full of bullshit write-ups. Understand?" I say, trying to get the kid to wake up. I get not wanting to wear the damn hat, but this kind of defiance is idiotic at best and career ending at worst.

He slowly reaches up and removes his baseball cap, or what could be seen as his security blanket. He nods his head before walking out of my office, leaving the door open behind him. He's gone before I can yell at him to close it. I'm trusting that kid to try to get me some more information to go on before I bring the boss into this. I'd rather handle it myself so Chase doesn't have the spotlight on him again.

The caller said that I wasn't safe and neither was my son. That confuses me a bit. One, everyone knows anyone working for the force can be touched, beaten, or killed. We're always out in the open. Sure, we have the blue line, but if you want to get to us, it is a pretty easy thing to do. Secondly, the son part.

Fear races up my spine as reality sinks in. They have my cell phone number; they must have done some research on who I am. That means they know who Chase is. They assumed our relationship is that of mother and son, but in the end, it doesn't really matter. He might be in danger, and I've never had to think or worry about that before.

"You look like you could use a friend." I look up to see Frankie leaning against the doorframe of my office, her beautiful hazel eyes boring into mine like they always have. Her sandy blonde hair cascades down her shoulders as her smile brightens my day. She takes two steps into my office before closing the door behind her.

I open my mouth to say something, but she raises her hand, effectively shutting me up.

"Victor called me. He said you sounded different—not frantic, but too calm for his liking. I told him you have a tendency to sound that way in the morning before your coffee. He said it was a calm, scary tone and definitely not normal Jasmine. So, here I am," she finishes.

"Shouldn't you be at work?" I ask, trying to change the topic of conversation.

"I have a rather open schedule. A rarity in my line of work, but it happened so here I am." She sits on the end of my desk and smiles at me. "Unless you want me to leave?"

I take her free hand in mine and kiss it gently before placing it against my forehead. I miss her so much it hurts in every fiber of my being. She runs her other hand through my hair.

"You want to tell me what's going on?" she asks.

I sit up, but never let go of her left hand. I need to be touching her right now, like lightening to a metal rod.

"I got a phone call today," I say, looking at her hand in mine.

"Okay, that's rather innocuous. Who was this mysterious caller?" Her tone remains light; she's used to pulling information from me.

"I wish I knew. Then I would know how to handle it."

"You're going to have to give me more than that to go on."

I look up at her; confusion and worry is playing all over her face. I hate opening up, but maybe she can help me figure out what this individual wants. She might have seen the behavior before in one of her other clients. She's the doc; I'm just me.

"The call was from a private number. I was in front of Chase's school when it came through. They knew who we were and basically said we could be in danger," I say calmly.

"Could be or are? They're very different phrases, Jasmine." She looks at me, waiting for me to explain. She has the most expressive eyes I've ever seen, and it makes me want to tell her the honest truth.

"Something about not being untouchable; it really doesn't matter. I've got to pull Chase from school until I figure it all out," I say, confident with my decision.

I let go of her hand and reach for my desk phone. Frankie places her hand on top of mine and pulls my hand away. She grabs my other hand and holds both of my hands tightly.

"You need to slow down and think about this rationally," she says, slowly and softly as if trying to get me to calm down.

"Frankie, you're the shrink; you know how criminals act." If anyone knows the vile things a human being can do, it's her. She gets to listen to several people weekly tell her their darkest secrets, and here she is stopping me from taking action. We've both seen the outcome when someone wants to inflict pain on someone else. I feel the anger starting to rise up and overtake the nervousness.

"Yes, I do. However, taking him out of school before we know anything only has negative consequences," she says, still trying to remain calm. I can see she's beginning to lose her cool as well.

"That's right, because saving his life is a negative," I say much harsher than I intended, and I immediately regret it.

Frankie lets go of my hands as her face changes. Her compassionate look converts into a colder, harder look. She stands up, crosses her arms, and shifts her weight. I can't tell if she's getting defensive with me or just protecting herself. Whatever the result, I'm the cause, which was a point of contention in our relationship.

"I'm sorry. That was out of line, even for me. I'm just really out of my element here," I say, trying to rationalize my words and emotions.

"Don't worry about it. I got used to your temper a long time ago," she says calmly. Her voice is firm, never wavering, and it pushes my buttons. Something we're both very good at with each other.

"I don't have a temper," I quickly shoot back at a volume not suitable for my office or anywhere really.

"Case in point . . ." She stares at me, and I realize the two of us are at a similar impasse.

This is what our relationship has come to. Like Congress, two opposing parties with different perspectives, neither willing to compromise or yield to the other. It became a game after a while in the downward spiral. I usually struck first and waited for her to retaliate. It was easier than accepting help, just like now. Frankie shakes her head before walking to the office door.

"Frankie, I'm sorry. I shouldn't snap at you, and there's no excuse for it. I'm on edge right now, and I know you're just trying to help," I say softly, trying to get her to listen. Her hand slides off the doorknob, and I see her visibly inhale. "What are the negatives of pulling him from school?"

"He's still trying to understand and accept his parents' deaths. If you add this to his already strained psyche, he might break mentally and physically." She finally turns around to face me but holds her ground by the door. The distance seems to help us both find some safety from the triggers.

"Is this something I could help him deal with, or would it be the point of no return?" I ask. The kid's well-being is my main concern, even if I don't show it clearly enough.

"Doubtful." She raises her hand to stop me, knowing full well I was about to shove my foot in my mouth again. "You're barely taking care of yourself. I know you're not eating properly, you barely sleep, and from what I understand, you are bringing more than your share of work home. That's not coping with stress; that's hiding from it."

"I can't confirm nor deny those allegations, doctor," I say, falling back into my chair. The trusty trio must be talking to one another more regularly than I thought. I'm not hiding my emotions or depression well enough.

"There's also the option that the courts might not like you placing him in harm's way," she adds.

"I don't follow," I say. My voice oozes concern and some fear.

"You're his legal guardian, but not his biological parent. If there is any indication of child endangerment, they could have a representative of Child Protective Services show up. That might lead to a suspension of rights. They could take him away, even temporarily," she says seriously.

"Like the foster care system is better? Even on my worst day I'm a better parent than any of those other people out there. I make sure he's fed, has a roof over his head, and whatever else he needs." My tone changes as my voice rises in emotion. I feel tears flood my eyes at the thought of losing Chase, and I fight the raw display of emotion. Before I have a moment to think about it, Frankie pulls me into a firm hug.

The sudden and unexpected contact causes me to hold the air in my lungs. I can feel her hot breath on my neck. She tries to meet my gaze, but I turn away. As long as I've known her, I've never been able to meet her eyes when I feel inferior or afraid. I was raised to be strong, fierce, and fearless. I wasn't made for this weakness. I don't know how to face someone I find so brilliant and truly show her my flaws.

"Jasmine Marie, look at me." She almost whispers, but it does the trick. I call it the parental call when you're in trouble. It was a staple in my house with my mother.

I turn my head, and my brain shuts off. Before I can stop myself from doing something beyond stupid, my lips are firmly planted on hers. Her hands slide up my arms as mine find their way into her hair. As quickly as it began, it's over, her hands firmly pressing my shoulders back and away from her.

"I'm . . ." I start but don't finish the thought. Frankie's face is slightly flushed, but her eyes never leave mine.

"Don't. Unless you are truly sorry, don't say it anymore. We also can't do that anymore, Jasmine. We're not together." She lets go of my shoulders and takes a few steps away. She fixes her shirt before running her right hand through her hair. "Everything will be okay. You've been here before. What would you normally do when a witness is threatened?"

She turns the conversation back to work, and part of me is upset. I know she enjoyed that kiss as much as I did, but she's right about us not being together.

"I'd get them into protective custody immediately. If they needed to be moved to a safe house, that would be considered. Depends on how severe and credible the threat against them was," I say, trying to compose myself.

"That might be true, but you also know it isn't applicable in every case. You once told me that hiding in plain sight was sometimes the best option. So, what do you do in a lower profile case where there isn't as much evidence to back up the threat?" she says, leading me to the rational conclusion.

"Notify the department of a possible threat. Tail the witness at all times, but keeping a safe distance so as to not alert those around them or the individual themselves," I answer, sounding more professional than emotional.

"So, what's stopping you from notifying the captain of your phone call?"

"I don't have anything to go on yet. I have an officer trying to pull information from my cell phone as we speak," I answer.

"You've taken steps to protect yourself, but you can't do this alone. Chase might not need a tail because of you, but he might need eyes."

"I can contact the principal and see if school security can keep tabs on him. make them aware so they can watch for anyone getting too close or looking out of place on the grounds," I continue with Frankie's train of thought.

"If you're running late, Victor, Hadley, or I will pick him up. That way he's never out of anyone's sight. If something goes wrong, you're always a phone call away. Trust yourself to handle this in a calm and efficient manner. Don't make it worse by flying off the handle like a new parent."

"I'm not a new parent. I've been around the kid since he was born. Hell, he peed on me when I changed his diaper for the first time. I'm the cool aunt who takes him everywhere and sugars him up. I'm not the one who carried him for nine months and popped him out in fifteen hours of natural childbirth. I'm just the aunt," I hurriedly ramble.

"But you are, sweetie. You have to make decisions for him that a parent normally would. These very choices will change his everyday life. Maybe not right away, but he will remember the changes. He might yell at you five years from now saying you ruined his life because of something you decided to do now. That's being a parent. It's so much more than which take out place is serving dinner tonight." Frankie brings it right back to the point at hand. This is the first time my decision will truly affect him. All the others were simple choices: school was in the district, clothing, shoes . . . all of it. Basic. This is his safety, and I'm not quite comfortable with it.

"You're right. About everything," I say, my voice barely above a whisper.

I look up at her standing by the door, and it hits me what I've really lost. It felt so natural to kiss her, to hold her, but in reality, she's just out of reach. I walk up to her and hold my hand out in front of her. She hesitates but places her right hand in my left. I simply lift it up and place it over my beating heart. She looks at our hands and then up to my eyes and smiles. My silent message got across exactly how I meant it.

Someone knocks on the office door, forcing Frankie to pull away from me. I take a few steps away from her and nod. She pulls the door open, revealing Officer Garrison standing next to an unhappy-looking Captain Tyler Udall.

"Doctor Ryan, what brings you here?" Udall asks professionally.

"A personal matter, but it's been handled. I have an appointment, so if you'll all excuse me." Frankie turns and walks out of the room before I can say anything. One thing she has is speed. I know firsthand from when she decided to move out. One minute the closet was full and the next it was half bare. When she decides on something, she does it. No more analyzing.

"Officer Garrison, Captain Udall, how may I help you both?"

The two men walk in. Garrison closes the door behind them, and Udall holds a file in his right hand. I already know this isn't a courtesy call, but I hope it's not what my gut is telling me.

"I found something on your phone. I know you requested it be under wraps, but it would go against protocol," Garrison states simply.

Sadly, my gut was accurate. The kid rarely ever follows the rules, which is why I asked him to handle it. I'm not sure if he's trying to throw me under the bus or earn brownie points with the boss. Either way, the kid is on my radar now.

I motion for the two of them to sit down. I keep my anger in check as I sit behind my desk. The information he has might be important to the safety of my charge, so I have to suck this up and play nice for a moment or two. Garrison places my cell phone back on my desk. He does it slowly but with purpose. Maybe to show he has control over the situation I'm currently in, or to drag out a process he thinks will reflect poorly on me.

I pick up the phone and scan the outside, seeing various smudges or fingerprints. I make a show of cleaning the phone off on my pants leg while staring at the young officer. When that's done, I open up the back. I remove the SIM card, memory card, and battery. I look it over, ensuring nothing nefarious has been added before putting the phone back together again. Once that's done, I power it back up.

"What did you find, Officer?" I say with a professional edge I didn't know I had in me.

"The individual who called you wanted you to find out where the call originated from. There was no attempt to hide the location or make it difficult to find. In fact, it was a landline call from an old warehouse in Harlem. It's an office building now, but according to the schematics on-line they have a fallout shelter in the basement," Garrison says proudly.

"And how does this connect to my caller?" I ask.

"I took it upon myself to check the various places in the building. None have protected phone lines, except one in the shelter itself. It was set up as a private line only to be used in case of emergency," he smugly finishes.

The captain leans over my desk and places a file in front of me. I slide it around so I can easily read it. I wait for the boss to explain what this has to do with everything. I know I've irritated him by asking a fellow officer to handle a personal matter without telling anyone. I don't need to throw gasoline on the fire.

"I figure since you were busy covering up the use of city payroll on personal matters, I would take it upon myself to investigate the location," he says. That means Garrison went to him immediately after finding out the location. The million-dollar question is why. He could have easily walked across the hall and handed it to me. Maybe Frankie and I could have used the distraction.

"I appreciate that," I say, trying to sound thankful rather than condescending.

"There happened to be a unit around the corner on lunch. Once they clocked back in, I had them investigate your fallout shelter. They found the body in the middle of the room. According to the coroner, liver temp gives us a time of death estimate of about twenty-four hours ago."

"In other words, he killed the guy in advance, dumped the body, and waited for the perfect time to call you," Garrison interjects.

"Thank you for stating the obvious, Officer Garrison. Did you manage to figure that out all by yourself or did the computer help you?" I answer, bringing his ego down a peg or two.

"Excuse me?" he nervously responds, and I'm thankful I found his weak point. Regardless of how he came to be in my office, trying to show you are better than a superior is out of line. If the boss wants to rip me apart, I'll handle it. This little shit has no right, nor authority, to do so. Especially when the case somehow has ties to my family. I will lash out and continue to do so if it protects those I love. Looking at his defeated face, I have no urge nor desire to apologize. That's a first.

"Officer Garrison, I think that's all for now. If you would, please go back to your desk. I appreciate you bringing this to my attention," the captain says without ever looking at the officer.

Garrison waits for a few seconds, as if to argue with the boss. Ultimately, he stands and pushes his shoulders back. He's trying to look dominant, but he looks like a kid trying to play with the big boys. He gives me a sly smirk which tells me everything I need to know. He exits my office and leaves me alone to face the music.

"Sir . . ." I begin, but the captain's face tells me to shut up. So, I do.

"You should have come to me, Jasmine," he says, sincerely worried.

"I assume Garrison shared the conversation with you?" I ask.

"No. Let's just say you and Doctor Ryan aren't as quiet as you think," he says.

"I was going to come to you once I had more information. Garrison was out of line talking to you first," I nonchalantly reply as I try to cover my ass from whatever I've done.

"In your opinion he was, but in mine he did the right thing. Someone called you and threatened your family, Jasmine. This is not something to take lightly."

"I'm not, sir. I also think Garrison has ulterior motives, like a detective's badge for example," I huff in annoyance. In truth, it's not that far from the reality of the situation. That's why I chose the kid in the first place.

"Either way, you should have come to me before speaking to anyone. Until further notice, I'm ordering Chase to be shadowed. Once information is brought to light, we will reevaluate the situation," he says firmly. I'm sure he can tell I'm not happy about his decision, but he leaves no room for negotiation. He's laid down the law, and that's the end of it. I've never been one to stand idly by and let someone dictate anything to me, regardless of their intentions. No one knows you better than yourself. I call it a flaw in the design of me as a person. Frankie refers to it as my fight-or-flight instinct.

"Tyler." I say his first name softly. "Frankie and I discussed it, and I don't want him knowing anything. He's too vulnerable right now." I lean back in my chair, cross my legs, and try to look as cool as a cucumber.

"I'm not surprised you spoke to her before bringing this to me, but rest assured the shadow will be just that," he soothes.

I remember that tone. He used it when I was a rookie making silly mistakes. My sister-in-law was best friends with his niece, so he's been there for me through thick and thin. He knows when to stop me from going off the deep end. This soothing voice is step one in the switch to calm me down. I also know it's when we start to negotiate the terms to a middle-of-the-road compromise.

"Okay, but I want to look over the crime scene, see if he left anything for me to find," I say simply.

"This might not be connected to the other two, Jazz. It doesn't fit the profile," he replies.

"If the signature's the same, it's connected. The call still originated from the area, and I should take a look at it," I answer, a bit more annoyed than before.

"Figure out the signature first. Then we'll see. This could be a random freak you put away years ago that is coming back now. We've all got one, two, or fifty of those." Udall stands up, opens the door to my office, and walks into the cacophony of noise from the day shift.

"Like you said, we'll see," I mumble to no one.

Picking up my coffee cup, I see it's empty. We might be lowly law enforcement, but our precinct has the best coffee in all of Manhattan thanks to the captain's heroics. I get up and head to the coffee machine.

I can feel eyes focusing on me as I move through the main areas. Word must have traveled faster than an epic fail video on YouTube. I can hear the whispering as I fill up my mug in the break room. I feel the shame creeping up from my chest to my face. Now they all know I'm weaker than they previously thought. Now they see my vulnerabilities. The world is closing in, and I need air—now. Picking up the pace, I break free from the double doors and inhale deeply, my coffee forgotten.

I look at my watch and see time has slipped from me once again. I have too much work to do and scheduling is an issue for me. Unlocking my rubbed clean phone, I dial Frankie.

"Hey." Simple yet effective opening, I guess. I can hear the concern in her voice.

"I know I don't have a right to ask, but can you do me a favor?"

"Name it," she says.

"Pick up Chase from school and stay with him. Turns out the call originated from the scene of a murder. I need to figure out as much as I can today. Might be late."

"I'll bring something to sleep in," she answers.

"I might not be that late."

"Jasmine, when your mind is focused on something it means you'll be very late." She slightly laughs through the phone and the butterflies swarm in my stomach again. I know she's right. Sometimes, I get so hung up on a case that I'm out all night. It might be Friday, and other people have the weekend to look forward to, but for me it never ends. There are no breaks between my brain and the cases sitting on my desk. I need to give closure to those people on the other side of the crimes. Give them something I still desperately need. That's been my driving force since the accident, to the detriment of my relationship and time with the nephew.

"Right. Chase has a set of keys," I tell her.

"It's okay . . . I still have mine," she whispers through the phone.

The unspoken elephant in the room rears its ugly head again. She's never made any attempt to give me her keys back. In return, I've never asked for them. It made everything so final, and if we ignore it, it isn't.

"Good." I force the emotion down into the deepest part of my chest. I have to lock it all up tight so I can function. It's the only way I know how to deal with this.

"If you want, I'll leave them with you when you get back," she offers half-heartedly.

"No," I quickly answer before my brain can process anything. "Since you offered to help with Chase, it only makes sense, right?"

"Okay, in case of emergencies. I understand," she says in her business tone. She doesn't understand, and I haven't been able to explain it either. Relationships involve communication, and right now we're both stranded on an island trying to decipher smoke signals. The only problem is the wind blows them to bits.

"I owe you." *More than you could ever know*, I say to myself.

"I'll see you in the morning."

No goodbye, just a click. Just like that she's off the phone. It could be because she knows my mind is focused on something else, but she could have said goodbye. I wonder if we've fallen apart so badly that simply saying goodbye is difficult. I can't think about this right now. After going to my office, grabbing everything, and locking up for the day, I head to the garage, hop in my car, and turn it on. The radio blasts to life, and I am off to the crime scene. I need to see it for myself. Regardless of what the boss says, there has to be something there.

Chapter Three

The war continues to rage on in my head, and I seem to be incapable of turning it off. Sounds from the outside world, like the glass bottle exploding beneath my tires, barely registers in my mind. It must have been a beer bottle. There are a lot of homeless in the neighborhood. They have a propensity to collect the bottles for spare cash. Some also drink to forget their world. Pulling up to the front of the building, I throw the car in park and exit.

The doorman stands out front and stares at me. Based on the report I skimmed through, the cops are long gone. I'm not sure why they left so quickly. Normally when a body is found, there are various levels of investigations beyond retrieval. The techs come in, detectives, everyone gets eyes on the scene to make their own conclusions. If nothing else, it's held until things can be processed properly back at the station. Regardless, I have to face mister doorman to get my way.

"Excuse me, I'm Detective Steele. I need to see your basement," I say as I dig out my badge and wave it at him.

"I'm sorry, but I can't let you down there," he says, unmoving.

I try to plead my case. "Yes, you can. A man was murdered last night, and I need to survey the scene. While I understand you're the door-man—"

He cuts me off rather rudely. "I wish I could help you." His stare is defiant, and if I was anyone else, I might turn around and run away. My rational mind would tell me to come back and fight another day, but not today. The one thing I have over big muscle doorman is simple–a gun. I have yet to ever pull the trigger except in training, but it looks very powerful, even in the holster.

"Sir." I slide my hand along my belt and let him see my gun. "I really do need to see the scene."

His eyes glance toward my trump card, and I do my best to fight my smile. I feel like I should sing Queen's "We Are the Champions," only with the word "I" instead of "we." This is where he should slowly step away from the door and allow me access to the basement.

"Like I said, Detective, I can't help you. I have explicit instructions." He smiles smugly at me.

Okay, time to pull out some backup and hopefully get some answers as to why I can't get in. Grabbing my cell phone from my pocket, I dial the boss. He answers on the third ring.

"Steele, where are you?" he asks.

I answer his question with one of my own. "Tyler, what's up with the scene? I need to get inside and look around."

"No can do," he says as he bangs his keyboard.

"What? You said I could see the scene myself and determine the signature," I say defiantly. He said it in my office: find a signature. That's what I'm here to do.

"No, I said you need to find the signature before going to the scene. You booked out of here like you always do when your mind is made up. If you had waited a freaking second, I would have told you we released it. They have a security company protecting all the entries. If something comes up, they call."

"Why? There could have been—"

"Nothing. There was nothing but a body. We took photos, there were no forensics, and we got pressure to release it. That's what we do when there's no money in the budget and a wiped-clean scene."

I turn my back to the doorman, taking in all of his tattoos. I wonder if he's killed someone with his biceps or if they are just for show.

"So, the body was dumped? If the private security is so good, how the hell did the killer get access?" I ask, getting more irritated by the minute.

"That's where those detective skills of yours come in." I hear what sounds like his fist hitting the keyboard. "Stupid computer! Steele, just give me a reason to get you inside and I'll do it. Otherwise, it's not an option."

I hit the end call button on my phone and take in the surrounds. Nothing pops out at me except the UFC doorman who continues to make me feel like a piece of meat.

"If there's nothing else, Detective, you need to leave the property," he says, flexing his neck and making one of his tats to look like its moving.

"Who has access to the basement?" I ask, standing my ground.

"I don't know. People come and go from the building all the time."

"It's an office building. You're telling me you don't recognize the same people going in and out day after day? I'm sure you have an idea of who uses the fallout shelter or not."

"I'm just the man at the door, lady," he answers with a smile.

I'm sure he's part of that private security bullshit that I'm not allowed to deal with. No one that big works the door. Most people would be afraid to go to work if he was at the door. Something isn't right.

I try a different tactic. "Who rents the floors?"

"City owns it." He finally gives me an answer to something.

"Wait. You're telling me that New York City owns the actual building or rents the office space?"

"All of it. They bought it, developed it, and moved their people in," he holds the door open for someone with a badge on their chest.

"Which department?"

"Up my ass and to the left." I guess I asked one question to many.

"Well, I always thought everything went to the right so you might want to get that checked out. Let me know if they find your head with it," I answer curtly with a smile.

"With all lack of respect, you need to leave before I'm forced to remove you. In other words, get into your gas-guzzling machine and drive away. You're blocking our driveway." He takes two steps toward me, and I raise my hands in surrender. Reaching into my pocket, I grab the remote starter and turn my truck on. I watch his expression go from firm to exasperated. I can tell he's got his undies in a twist from me wasting gas.

"I'll see you around." I turn and head to the car. "Before I go, have you ever done time? Don't lie to me. I can easily look you up later."

"One stint when I was younger," he says, moving back to his original place by the doors.

"That explains it then." I grin as I walk to the driver's side and open the door.

"Explains what?" he calls after me.

I don't bother with a reply, but I smile at him as I slide into the car. I can tell by the doorman's face he's not happy with my lack of explanation. Looking at the clock, I see it's later than I'd like. Chase should be home. Placing the Bluetooth in my ear, I dial the house.

"Hello?" Frankie's melodic voice fills my ear.

"Frankie, it's me."

"Who else would it be?"

"You never know."

"Calling from Steele, J. cell?" She laughs into the phone. "I know you're a little worried, but caller ID still functions."

"Okay, so you knew it was me this time. What if next time someone has my phone?" I'm frustrated, and I know my playful tone does nothing to hide it.

"Then I would be worried that someone had your phone. I would dial the captain with my cell phone while I kept whoever it was on the phone. The entire time, I would be praying that you weren't harmed. Now, seeing as you were the other person on the line, it leads me to believe you are uninjured. You still don't sound happy, though. What happened?"

"I was denied entry into a crime scene. Apparently, they picked up the body, took some photos, and released it. Something's not sitting right with me. I'm headed back to the office to flesh it out. The city apparently owns and inhabits the building, but I need to know who has access to the basement," I rattle off.

"That's a lot of information to process. Could take you all night. Have you spoken to Victor?" she asks.

"Not yet. He's probably behind schedule in autopsy anyway."

"I'd stop by and see him first. Worst case, it's a wasted elevator trip. Maybe he's managed to look over the victim's body and can give you an idea of what they went through."

"I will. Still have to go over the case file and figure out what led them to quickly release the scene."

"That does seem out of character," she adds to my train of thought.

"City owned and budget cuts. That pretty much sums it up," I say bitterly.

"Find out what you can. When you get home, we'll talk it through. Maybe there's enough for me to build up a profile on your perp."

"You don't have to do that. I know you're busy with your patients. You don't need to add this unofficial case to the menu."

I hear her take a deep breath as if weighing her options. Frankie is one of the most amazing psychologists in all of Manhattan. She has a schedule that rivals mine, and she works fewer hours. No matter how much I want her to help, I can't expect her to.

"Yes, I'm busy dealing with patients and various trial dates. I still want to help. Besides, I'm already here. What's a few hours working on cases like we used to?" I can hear a little bit of hopefulness in her voice, and it makes my shoulders feel lighter.

"I'd appreciate that. Truthfully, I don't even know if they're tied together. I just need one shred of evidence and I'm golden."

"One step at a time, grasshopper. You can't put the horse before the cart."

Silence falls between us, but it's nothing like before. There's a comfort to it, an understanding. I used to handle it better when it was just me. I was always alone, so the quiet was just that. I never analyzed it. Then I met Frankie and being alone wasn't as nice as it used to be. Now I have Chase. The house would be deathly empty without him in it. Plus, no kid noise means he's up to something.

"Just a quick note; you have a shadow." I let her know of the detectives following Chase around.

"I know. They followed us home." She's so much smarter than most people give her credit for.

"Did Chase see them?"

"I don't think so. If he did, he's certainly not bothered by it," she answers.

"Just keep an eye on him for me, okay?"

"I will." Silence once again. This time it's uncomfortable. I can feel that damn elephant again. Mustering all the strength I have inside the core of my being, I say, "Frankie, about earlier in my office. I think we need to—"

"I'll see you when you get back. Just bring all the papers to your house and we'll figure it out."

Click. Once again, there's no goodbye. The dismissal of my suggestion boils over into instant rage. I let it out as I pound my steering wheel sitting at a red light. No more tears are left to fall. All I have is stress, anger, loss, and unadulterated fear of the unknown in front of me. A few horns honk behind me, and I'm forced to calm down and drive. It's hard being in control of yourself all the time. It's hard to hide the emotions and pretend they don't affect you.

I open my phone and dial Chase's school. Might as well warn them of the other people on campus.

"PS Two Eighty-Four."

"Hello, this is Detective Jasmine Steele. My—" I stop abruptly, trying to figure out how I should refer to my nephew. At this point he's technically mine, but he's not really mine when it comes down to it.

"Hello?"

"Yes, sorry. Chase Steele attends your school and recently some information's come to light that requires a protective detail. They've been instructed to be very inconspicuous. You won't even notice them."

"Detective, please have them come to the main office to show proper identification and paperwork. Then we will decide how they can fit into the current staff correctly."

"Thank you very much."

"You're welcome."

Disconnecting the call, I wonder why it was so easy. Maybe they've dealt with this kind of thing before, or maybe they think I'm a prank caller. I do question why I let the school decide how the officers are going to fit in. This is an ongoing investigation; they should allow me to place my men in their school however I see fit. Yet, I relinquished that right rather easily.

Pulling into a parking spot, I throw the hands-free device into the center console and grab the police file. Hopping out of the car, I watch as a few officers stare at me as I enter the other section of our building. It's as if they expect me to be fired after one mistake. Either that or word has gotten out about the threat against my family. It's as if Chase came to live with me and I became weak. I'll never understand how strong women who do their jobs are bitches with no emotion, and women with kids suddenly have no backbone. Men can jerk off into a cup and be called a man no matter what. It's not that hard to donate the seed; try carrying the fucking kid for once.

"Thinking to yourself again?" Victor questions my zombie-like stare.

"Not really. Just thinking. What've you got, Victor?" I ask as he finishes stitching up his *Y* incision in a dead man's chest.

Victor drops the needle onto the side tray and pulls off his gloves. He looks like shit as he covers up the body in front of me.

"A migraine. You?" He rubs his temples as if that's going to help the pain subside. I look over to his desk and see a stack of files. Maybe the caseload has been too heavy for him. He's been doing way too many jobs these last few years. Hopefully, they'll hire someone else to do the science stuff and just let him cut people open. Regardless, he always seems to have answers for me when I need them. Just don't touch that desk or chair of his to find said answers. Those are sacred places covered in papers.

"Indigestion," I answer.

"Fast food?"

"No food."

"Even better. There's some yogurt in the fridge." He points with his free hand to a small fridge across the room.

I gag. "How you manage to keep food in a room filled with death is beyond me."

"I'm not the one who had a chicken wrap at a blood-spattered crime scene."

"It was once and I was starving," I reply, splitting hairs.

"Whatever you say, Jazz."

Victor moves to his desk and fumbles around with a few things before grabbing something. He hands me the file and I flip it open. The pictures are clear, organ weights and other information I can make out. The chicken scratches prove to be a bit too difficult to comprehend.

"Are you going to tell me about the vic or do I have to attempt the translations? Cause if so, I'm fucked," I say, holding the gibberish out for him to see.

"Female victim. Estimated time of death was twenty-four hours before she was found. She was strangled like the others."

"That's it?" I ask.

"Based on the bruising around her neck, it appears as if she was strangled first and then mutilated. If there was any chance our victim was still alive, the blood loss would have killed her in seconds."

"Like she wasn't dying fast enough. One had to finish the job quickly. Maybe they were interrupted," I say to myself.

"Everything matches the other victims in regard to height, hair color, and eye color. Their ages are all in the same range," Victor continues, ignoring me.

"Whoever did this has a specific look and desire."

"The chest was severely damaged during a struggle. There were several stab wounds tearing the skin almost totally off. However, there was significant damage to the bones directly under the breasts." Victor pulls back the sheet and shows me the poor woman's flesh.

It's a horrible sight. From the breast area down are any number of slices and rips to the tender flesh. None of them are overly deep, but the skin has been pulled off in sections. This woman was tortured to death and removed of everything that made her human.

"So, we can make an assumption that these are all connected, but without a signature or a method to their madness, we only have theories. I need something solid," I plead.

"You know, the more I look at the victims, the more they all look like Hadley," he says with a bit of worry in his voice.

"You're personalizing it, Victor," I say, but in the back of my mind, I think he's onto something.

"Point taken," Victor concedes.

"Any ideas on a common denominator?"

"Other than looks and similar patterns in the cause of death, nothing yet."

"That's got to be our priority," I say firmly to make my point.

Victor stares at me like a smacked puppy, and I watch it turn into a far-off look. He does this often when he's thinking but doesn't want to share. It's like being a Met fan sitting in the middle of Yankee Stadium. He walks over to his desk and begins organizing the papers. He knows full well I'm still there and he wants me to initiate the conversation. He has passive-aggressive behavior down perfectly.

"I know you're waiting for me to ask. What's on your mind?"

"Nothing." He tosses one file onto a larger pile as if he doesn't want to tell me.

"There's something going on in that brain of yours, Victor."

"You're not going to want to hear it."

I'm not sure what's worse at the moment. Frankie ignoring me when I finally decide to talk about kissing her in my office or my best friends who always think they know what's best for me. Not only that, but they refuse to tell me anything for fear that I can't handle it in my fragile state. According to the shrink, I'm okay to handle vicious murder cases but not simple things. I know I've been through the wringer in the last few years, but the fact that I haven't put my gun in my mouth shows I can handle a lot.

Victor sits on the edge of his desk watching me. I know he's waiting for me to ask again, but I'm not playing the game this time. Maybe it's because I'm emotionally drained, but my gut tells me it's because I really don't want to hear it. I've got a file to read and a profile to create, so I'm going to walk away from this situation. I turn and head to the door.

"Since you asked."

"I asked for this soon-to-be lecture?" I roll my eyes.

"Your facial expressions begged me to speak." He smiles at me as his tone drips with sarcasm.

"Ah yes, the back of my head spoke volumes," I counter.

"More than you know; trust me, the scalp tells all." Victor points to the head of a dead body on a slab. "You need to hear this, like it or not."

"Remind me to get a different, less vocal haircut and color."

He reaches into his desk drawer and pulls out two small glasses and a bottle of brandy. Without missing a beat, he stands and places them all on an occupied slab. Normally, I'd be a bit grossed out by this. Not right now. I'm sure this conversation isn't going to be an easy one. We do one shot before he fills mine up again. I take another shot and place the glass down. He fills the two up once more and closes the bottle.

"Where's Chase?" He leans back on his desk, brandy in hand.

"With Frankie." I take a sip this time, using the alcohol as a distraction.

"At your place?"

"No, they're at my mother's." I take a gulp of brandy this time, the burning in my chest reminding me I'm alive and dealing with the here and now.

"I doubt the cemetery has a hotel on the premises. She's dead; try again."

"Aren't we all?" I say before my mind can block the comment.. I take a long swig of the brandy and try to focus on the glass in my hand. I peer through my eyelashes and see Victor watching me.

"You have to deal with it eventually, Jasmine. You can't keep hiding behind that facade for much longer."

"I've got Chase. We're cool," I lie. We're not cool, but I don't air my dirty laundry if I can help it.

"You haven't been cool since we were in our twenties." He drains the rest of the glass before pouring another one. He leans over and fills my glass to the top again.

"College wasn't what it could have been. It was . . . harder than I anticipated." I fight the emotion filling me from the toes up.

"No one expected her to die." The sincerity in his voice causes me to crack a little.

"I did. You can deny it all you want, Victor. We watched her give up. We all let her do it. Simple as that." My voice cracks as a few tears spring free from my eyes. Quickly wiping them away, I look anywhere but at the man in front of me. This is not how I wanted my day to go.

"Jazz, we've known each other for a long time. I know when you're full of shit." His eyes stay firmly planted on me. He can see right through my lies, but not as easily as Frankie. Most of the time I let him think he's right, even if he's way off base. Today though, he's right on target.

"And I know when you're trying to get me to admit shit. Victor, Mom died. It sucks. I miss her, but she's dead and there's nothing I can do about it. So, drop it." I drink again. I don't like to indulge this much, but I need to feel something, anything, and the burning liquid does just that.

His eyes never leave me, but he stands there, speechless. He's not used to having me give him information without him needing a crowbar. He nods at me as if thinking of his next chess move. I meant what I said, but I think I caught him off guard. We never really talk about Mom. He asks, but I ignore the questions. Victor was there for all of it: her aging, the pain, and the lack of desire to live. I can still see her face looking up at the ceiling, empty.

At eighty years old, she would just lie in bed and drift away mentally. She used to escape with books or a long hot bath, but eventually I lost her to nothingness. I would beg and plead with her to get up, but she chose not to. She wasn't sick. She wasn't terminal. She just had no desire to live—not for me, not for Chase's family, not for herself. One day I tried to bring her coffee to encourage her to get up and her body was ice cold. Hell has a way of creeping into your pretty world and smashing it all to bits. One day I had a mother and the next I was a mother. Hell has burned me and continues to fry me every chance it gets.

"Have you moved on?" he asks gently.

"Have you heard from your soon-to-be-ex lately?" I answer angrily, the pain evident in my voice.

"Why do you answer everything I ask with a question?" His shoulders pull back in a defensive position, and I know I'm pushing all the wrong buttons, but I don't stop.

"Because it pisses you off," I reply harshly.

"Jazz, you're an asshole sometimes." He downs his drink and walks over to the sink.

"I've been called worse."

"Usually by me." His back remains to me as he cleans the glass. He's being overly methodical, and I don't know if it's because he's really hurt or he's sizing me up. "Nice necklace," he throws at me.

I'm sure the confusion on my face is clear as day. I fumble around my neckline until I touch the familiar gold cross on a chain.

"I see you still wear it."

"Every day. You know that." I'm getting fidgety and play with the glass in my hand. It's almost empty, like everything else around me. Victor was right; this is not a conversation I want to continue. I didn't really want to start it either. In a perfect world, I would be able to run home and crawl into my mother's loving arms, but I can't.

Victor places the glass next to the jars filled with human organs. He turns and leans against the counter as he dries his hands.

"Look, I'm going to just say it like it is. You're a good guardian for Chase and eventually you will learn to be a good mother. Those things take time, but you have to figure out your priorities and get your life on track."

It's an amazing gift to make the voices around you blur into nothing. I've done it since I can remember. Parents fighting, teachers and coaches yelling—you name it, I can ignore them. All the words and sounds blend together like an orchestra, and I am the conductor. The only difference is I prefer not to hear it. Let the audience enjoy it, but I prefer the sound of silence.

"Stop ignoring me." He raises his voice to get my attention.

"You want me to stop ignoring you, fine. Let me say it like I know it is. I will not be a good mother. I will never be able to replace his birth mother, nor will I ever attempt to. I am only who I can be, and that's not much. Simply put, I am an individual who is drowning in responsibilities that I never asked for. I allowed the individual I loved more than my own life to walk away due to said responsibilities." I try to control my breathing, but I feel my heart racing with every breath.

"You never lost her." He tries to calm me, but that battle has been lost already.

"You had your turn. Now it's mine." I swallow the rest of the brandy and slam the glass on the slab. It might have cracked or broken; I don't know and I don't care. Victor is watching me intently now, his face mixed with fear and surprise at my actions.

"I did lose her, Victor. Fuck, I kissed her in my office, and she just ignores that it happened." I watch the shock form on his face before I continue. "You want to know how I feel about my mother? She died. She left me. I watched her waste away to nothing under the pressures of responsibility. She took care of everyone as they all died. Grandma, Grandpa, my father . . . she took care of them all. I had to sit and help. I had to watch her die inside a little each day while she cleaned up after my father. I was no perfect angel, but I know how life beats you down. How you eventually look at yourself in the mirror and you are no longer the woman you thought you were.

"She gave up. Once my dad died, she had a chance to finally live her life. Instead, she faded away. I couldn't help her. I couldn't protect her. I abandoned her when she needed me most. So, who failed who? Did she fail me by going to sleep and desiring never to wake up? Did I fail her by allowing her to give up so easily? I don't know. My heart tells me I should have pushed harder for her, yet my anger tells me that she gave up on herself. So, doctor, you figure it out. In the meantime, I have responsibilities to deal with."

Before another word can be said, I am out the door and out of this argument. I hear him walking behind me, but I don't entertain the idea of turning around. I don't have the emotional capacity to handle everything in one shot. I feel wetness hit my cheeks, and I know the tears are flowing freely now. They are a sign of weakness, but right now I couldn't give a shit. I wipe the tears on my shirt so I can actually see.

Thankfully, the house is quiet by the time I get home. I leave the lights off as I empty my pockets and hang up my coat. Moving into the living room, I try to navigate the maze to the couch.

"Fuck," I mumble, hopping on one foot with papers in my hand.

Somehow off balance, my only good leg hits the couch, and I careen backwards, dropping everything in my hands to the floor. I slam my head against the cushions in aggravation. The photos and papers will have to be sorted again. I reach over and turn on the light next to me. Rubbing the back of my neck, I see a pair of sweatpants and a baggy shirt folded on the coffee table. Frankie remembered I think better in my sleepwear. Oxymoron it might be, but it's a fact of my existence. I quickly change out of my clothes and instantly feel better.

Slowly making my way down the hall, I see Chase's door slightly ajar. Usually, I close it all the way, but I guess with me not being home he wanted it open. I push it open ever so slightly so it doesn't creak. He's lying on his side facing the wall. His chest rises and falls in a nice rhythm. I'm surprised he stayed in his bed, but he was really upset when Frankie left. Maybe he wants to keep his distance so he doesn't get hurt again. If that's the case, I wouldn't blame him.

My bedroom door hangs slightly open as well. I wonder if Frankie remembers those times he climbed into bed with us. I peek inside and see Frankie sleeping soundly on my side of the bed. My feet have a mind of their own, and I don't fight them. Sitting on the edge of the bed, I watch her sleep peacefully. I used to love the times I would wake up hearing her talk to me, yet she was sound asleep. Before my brain can consciously focus on what I'm doing, my fingers slide down the side of her face. Her skin feels exactly how I remember. I don't think there was anything I didn't love about this woman. If only that was enough.

Exhaling a breath I had no clue I was holding, I stand and take one last look at my sleeping beauty. Time heals all wounds, but sometimes accepting fault also helps. I walk out of the room and close the door behind me. Getting back to the living room, I kneel down by the couch and pick up the photos. They have to be organized with the documents based on timelines and crimes. For some reason, my brain goes on autopilot again as I keep thinking about Frankie.

When I met her, everything was going okay in my life. I was in college looking for a new and exciting adventure. I was nineteen, writing was my dream, and Anne Rice was going to eat my dust. I had plans to do something in the future. I promised Hadley I was going to write her a part in a screenplay that would guarantee her an Oscar nomination at least. Now, the two of us struggle to stay afloat. I feel bad for letting her down, but life gets in the way.

Victor and I were sitting at a bar one night, and Hadley was running late as per usual. I was solely focused on the pool table and this hot woman playing with her friends. Victor and I were comparing notes. He thought the hot girl was a whore, and I disagreed vehemently. Turns out he was referring to the girl leaning down on the table with short shorts that barely covered her crack while I was talking about Frankie. Once we had it cleared up, Victor dared me to talk to her. I swore under my breath because I hated being forced to do anything, especially fail in public. I really wanted to talk to her; it seemed like a good excuse.

I accepted his terms, swallowed my shot of Patron, and headed toward the pool table. I was about ten paces in when Frankie leaned down over the short shorts girl and whispered in her ear. Considering how their hands were on the pool cue, I felt jealousy rage from everywhere inside me. I turned on a dime and went back to the bar. Victor had seen the whole thing and had three shots ready, one for him and two for me. Once Hadley showed her face, we did nothing but drink.

And drink. And drink. I did shots of crappy tequila when the Patron was all gone. I was so out of my mind, I even licked the salt off the hot bartender's abs, sucked the tequila from her naval, and then made out with her for the lemon. That's when things got a bit heated. Frankie walked up to the bar to order a few drinks. She leaned in-between me and Victor, which is like a sin in his world. So, he was giving her the look of death; it's a hysterical look when he's wasted. Me, I couldn't breathe. She was leaning on my leg without necessarily meaning to. I could smell the cigarette stench too, and it made me leave my stool and rush to the bathroom.

Next thing I know, I'm facing the toilet and Victor's holding my hair in the ladies' bathroom. When my stomach was finished, Victor, always the awesome wingman, handed me a piece of gum. I was sober after the evacuation of my insides, but the evening was going from bad to worse. Victor and I said our farewells to Hadley, who was too busy talking shop with a film student to do anything but wave.

Victor pointed to some side street and told me to meet him there, something about me stumbling into traffic. So, I walked around the building and came face to face with Frankie against the wall with the hot girl on her like a moth to a flame. I don't really know how long it took for realization to set in, but when Frankie's eyes met mine, she was pleading for help. I don't know how or why, but protectiveness took over. I tapped the hot girl on the shoulder and questioned what her intentions were with my girlfriend.

Frankie watched me cautiously. I'm sure she had no idea if I was another person coming to assault her or a Good Samaritan. The hot girl removed herself from Frankie and looked me up and down. I'm one tall, intimidating bitch when I want to be, and right then I wanted to be one. She puffed her chest out, and I just crossed my arms, flexing every muscle I have—all three of them. Eventually, after a few words were said, the bitch left and Frankie smiled at me. Victor honked the cabbie's horn, and I offered Frankie a ride home. I think I passed out on her shoulder. I remember feeling her fingers running through my hair. She has that comforting effect on anyone, regardless if she just met them.

We dated for about two years before moving in together. It just felt right. She was making a lot more money than I was, so she paid the majority of the rent. I took care of a lot of the basics, but struggling writers don't make much. So, when Frankie decided to take psychology classes at night, I went with her. At the time, I thought it would help me write my crime dramas or maybe a simple horror film. Truthfully, I had no idea that degree would change my life forever. We graduated. I became a cop and then a detective, mostly due to my degree, anal retentive studying, and having a great support staff around me.

Don't get me wrong, money has to be made to survive, so this job was a means to an end. I had book ideas on various Post-it notes, and they were posted everywhere. Frankie used to say my desk looked like it was hit by a sticky note explosion. I still wrote a lot at night, and Frankie worked while getting her doctorate. We were talking about our future and trying to figure out a way to secure our finances. Then, everything changed with one phone call.

It wasn't a call in the middle of the night. Not a rainy day. No snow. The sun had been out all day, and I was going to surprise Frankie at dinner. When the phone rang, I swore it was her. Happy as a clam, I answered with my usual "hello, love." It wasn't her. The officer on the other end asked me to come to a crime scene. I told him I was off duty and I would be in tomorrow. I assured him the officers on the clock were more than capable, but he still insisted I come down. I abandoned my plans and headed to the crash site.

Looking down, I see tears have actually fallen from my eyes and landed on the crime scene photos. Not a good thing. Quickly wiping them off the image, I see more spots form on my shirt. I lean back on my heels and look up at the ceiling. I just want to be able to stop for once in my life and smell the roses again. Brick by brick, I felt the walls go up around me. I didn't ask it to happen, but I never stopped it either. One by one, they stacked up higher and higher, preventing me from feeling pain or anger. I became someone who hid everything. I watched as my family died one at a time. I keep harping on it, but I know that's where it began. When the walls began building themselves up was when I began to lose myself.

I've been to enough shrinks to know that when I start to lose myself, I try to overcontrol the things I still have some handle on. Like my relationship with Frankie became cold and unwelcoming. It wasn't a safe haven for me anymore. In my head I knew she would leave somehow, and I couldn't control it. I know I was full of shit, but when everything is messed up in your head, these unrealistic thoughts are always crystal clear. I made it a self-actualizing prophecy. I shut down my heart and didn't let her help me through my mourning period.

Chase lived with us while my brother's paperwork was sorted out. I never knew how difficult death was on the rain forest. All those papers, signatures, and so many lawyers getting their hands in the cookie jar. Frankie tried to help me make sense of it all, but like I said, I shut down. She used to put papers in front of me and point to a line. I signed my name, and she would put the next document in front of me. Chase liked her, but he was in his own world as well. No matter how hard Frankie tried to help, we didn't let her. She moved out a little while later. I think she knew I needed to do it on my own, whether she was my life partner or not.

Next thing I knew, the papers were finalized and the courts officially handed me Chase. Me. A cop, failed writer, and villain chaser. A person who barely had her own footing beneath her, being told I had a son legally and I never gave birth to him freaked me out. I never thought they would trust me to be responsible for another human being. There I was in the courtroom responsible for a child that had the same walls built up around his heart that I did. We'd both lived through the same torment, just from a different perspective. The first time Chase held my hand and we walked to the car as guardian and child, we were both empty. His hand felt foreign in mine, like I was forced to hold it. No emotional attachment behind it, just hollow. I love him now as much as I did then, but we were both suffering, and nothing could break those walls down.

Since I couldn't really control my situation with Chase, I controlled what I could. Sleep rarely came to me, so I dove deep into work all hours of the night. I would make sure Chase ate and got to his new school. He didn't lack for anything he truly needed, and sometimes, when I had a little extra cash, I would get something special for him. We rarely spoke at all during the first few months he was here. Nothing to say, I guess.

I never ate either. Food always hit my stomach like lead sinkers burying themselves in an acid pool. Once it was down, it came back up. Maybe it was a mental thing, but I never had a stomach of steel like my brother. Instead of dealing with the pain of vomiting, cramps, indigestion, or whatever else, I just stopped eating. Frankie noticed it first but said nothing. Victor and Hadley yelled at me a lot. I just let the voices fade into nothingness. They start to sound like flies buzzing around your head. Frankie was the only voice I heard most of the time. She got me those canned shakes. Sometimes I remembered to drink one, sometimes I threw them up, but for her I tried.

I'll admit the walls are still up—crumbling, but still there. The day they began to fall was the day Chase crawled into my bed and finally let go. I was staring at the ceiling, thinking of the millions of ways I could have saved my brother and his wife. The door opened and he padded across the floor, saying nothing. He lifted the blankets and climbed into bed. He slid over to me and put his head on my shoulder. I remember my shirt being wet with his tears as he finally let his feelings show. I kissed the top of his head and said nothing. Just wrapped him in a hug, and for the first time in what felt like ages, I fell asleep.

Since then, he's grown a little more attached to me. He talks more and actually eats a full meal instead of pushing various items around his plate until I take it away. His eyes have more life to them as well, although I am not sure how much more they have to go to be normal. I don't know if it's even possible to be considered normal after all we've been through. Maybe someone can quantify it for me so I have a gauge of where we should be. No one ever does though. They tell you what you're feeling is okay and to face it. It's like asking someone to sit in a plane knowing it will crash just so they can deal with their fear of heights.

Realizing the papers are neatly sorted on the table, I sit on the couch. Staring at images of mutilation, at horrific sights, I find I have no emotion toward them. I don't think I'm normal. I can see these things on a daily basis and nothing boils in my chest. I used to let all these emotions wrap around me, consume me, and now—nothing. I wait, I stare, and nothing. Maybe it is normal to become desensitized to this sort of thing, but I wish I wasn't. Maybe I would feel more alive if these images bothered me. All I see as I stare at them is a poor victim in the wrong place at the wrong time. I see individuals who had their lives changed by a decision they thought was a benign one. That's why I keep asking myself what the fuck normal means.

Lying down on the couch, I place the photos on my chest. Maybe a closer look will allow me to see something . . . anything connecting them all together. Besides their appearance, nothing seems to jump out at me. All blonde, all blue eyes, all strangled, and all are dead. Bodies cleaned of evidence. No sexual assault. No nothing. I'm supposed to figure these things out, yet as I look at these images, it becomes increasingly impossible I might never find the person responsible for their deaths. I'm not angry or upset. I'm almost indifferent, but I do worry about the perp still being on the street. It's another irrational fear I've obtained over the years. Anything could hurt Chase, and I have to find a way to protect him from the bad guys. I love him with all of my heart, and frankly, I have come to accept I need him as much as he needs me.

Man, my head hurts just thinking about it. This meaning of life crap, the destiny, fate, and normal or abnormal—what the fuck does it all mean? I'm sure everyone has been through this, where you literally overthink shit that has no reason to be thought about at all. I mean hell, we all do what we have to do to survive, right? Yet, here I am thinking about things I cannot control. Why? Because I want to control them. I need to feel in control.

Chapter Four

Coffee: sweet-smelling coffee. The one thing that I can always count on is the deliciously addicting warm liquid to quench my early morning thirst. Not to mention it keeps my ass awake all day considering the restless nights I've had recently. If there was a way to stay awake, eliminating those nightmares, I would sign up in a heartbeat. Coffee just seems to quiet the brain for the daylight hours, which helps. My biggest concern is the creator of said brew. If it's the mischievous little nephew of mine, I face a morning of sludge sliding down into the pit of my gut. If it's not him, then I face Frankie, and I'm always awkward around her. Neither possibility is really appealing at the moment.

"I know you're awake," Frankie softly utters. "Your nostrils flare at the smell of freshly brewed coffee. Don't pretend you're asleep to hide from seeing me. Get up or I pour it on your head."

My eyes fly open at the threat, seeing a nice, steaming pot of coffee directly in front of my face. Frankie moves it before I sit up, hit my head, and spill said fluid all over myself. Not only would that be a waste, it would burn like hell.

"I'm awake," I mumble pathetically.

"Better. Good morning to you too." Frankie turns away and heads to the kitchen.

"Morning," I say a bit louder this time. I try to rub the sleep out of my eyes as well as the dryness from my contacts. Sitting upright, I look over the piles on the coffee table. Yawning, I stare at the various images, wondering where to begin.

Frankie walks back into the living room and places a full mug of coffee in front of me. I take a look at the mug she's chosen, and even in my tired state, I smile. It's the mug she bought me on our second anniversary. A massive, double-sized one with the words *Now Talk* at the bottom. She knows nothing gets done before my first cup. Her mug is a simple one with a faded image of a pug, my grandmother's.

"I assume you drink it the same," she says, and I nod in response. "You might also want to consider thinning out your mug collection."

"Please don't go there; it's too early," I mumble into the steam hitting my face. The overflowing cabinet has mugs from all over the world, all double sized, and most of them from family members long gone. To part with any of them would make me feel like I was throwing out a piece of them. I can't do it, and I won't talk about it.

"Okay." She drops the subject and takes a drink.

Swinging my legs over the edge of the couch, the pain shoots up my back and down my legs. I forgot how uncomfortable this thing is to sleep on, but sometimes the extremes are better than the means. Mindlessly, I massage the knot in my lower back as I prepare for the long day ahead.

"You should have come to bed." She places her mug down on one of the few areas free of my clutter and sits down beside me. Her hands find their way to the sore spot, and she gently rubs it.

"I didn't want to wake you," I reply through various winces of discomfort.

"You wouldn't have woken me. If you were concerned about something else"— she inhales deeply as if trying to find her thoughts—"that wouldn't have happened."

"It wasn't that. I know how hard it is for you to fall back asleep. That's all," I reply softly.

We hear the telltale signs of a tiny human getting up in his bedroom. Frankie moves to a chair next to the couch. The moment her hands leave my skin, it feels so cold.

"Maybe you should have a professional look at that," she says.

"Nah, then it goes on my medical record," I say, shrugging my shoulders.

"Do you have to work today?" I look over to see Chase in his dinosaur pajamas with the little feet attached. No matter how old he tries to act, now and then he does something that reminds me he's still a kid. As he stands there rubbing sleep from his eyes in full footy pajamas, I'm reminded of myself at his age.

"Yeah, little man. I have to work on this case," I say, tilting my head to the gaggle of papers on the table.

"Is it getting worse?" He climbs onto the couch with me, his eyes slightly red from lack of sleep. His head hits my chest, and I wrap my arm tightly around him. I kiss him on the head before looking over to Frankie, who has a large smile on her face. This is the type of mornings we had planned on back in the day. "Is it?" Chase asks again.

"Not so much worse as confusing the fu—"

Frankie cuts me off. "Watch your language."

"Sorry. It's really confusing me a lot, kiddo. I'm not quite sure where to start."

"Why do you do that?" He looks up at me.

"Do what?"

"Call me little man, then kiddo, and then tiny human?"

"I don't know. Just what comes out of my mouth, I guess." I smile at him and ruffle his hair a bit.

"Your Aunt Jazz has a tendency to give everyone a nickname. If you're lucky, you only get one. I think she has about four for me," Frankie adds with a hint of laughter in her voice.

"Okay, can we drop the tiny human one? Maybe all of them when I get older?" Chase asks with a bright smile on his face.

"I'll see what I can do. Can't promise anything. You know I have a bad memory," I tease.

"No, you're just old." I cannot believe he just said that. Looking in his eyes, he knows something's up. Before I can grab him for some much-deserved tickle torture, he's off running into Frankie's arms. "Ha, you can't catch me."

"Chase, my dear little man. You're in Frankie's arms." I lean back confidently.

"Yeah, so. She's the safety zone," he states calm as can be.

Sipping my coffee, I look back over to him and smile mischievously. "No, my dear little man; she's worse than I could ever be."

I see the change in his expression right away. He rolls his eyes up and sees Frankie smiling at him. In seconds he's giggling and rolling around in her arms trying to break free as she mercilessly tickles him.

"Stop," he says through gasps and laughter.

"Not until you say the magic words," she says to him.

"Please, Aunt Frankie." The words come out of his mouth and everything stops. I just stare at Chase, then Frankie, who looks like a deer in a set of headlights. She looks at me, a mixture of emotions oozing off her, but what they are I can't tell.

"Did I do something wrong?" Chase snaps me back to reality and to the situation at hand. "Is that okay?" he asks again fear rising in his voice.

"Is what okay?" I manage to squeak out. The words hang in the air, waiting for someone else to answer the question.

"Not you, Aunt Jazz," he replies simply.

There are moments when a child takes control of a situation and it's a learning experience for the parent. This is one of those times. Chase has chosen someone else to be a part of his family. I knew he liked her and was upset she left, but I never understood how much he must have cared for her. He only calls me Aunt Jazz; he calls everyone else is by their first names. This is a huge thing for him.

Chase wiggles out of Frankie's arms and manages to sit on her lap, his eyes full of innocence as he searches hers. "Is that okay?" he says softly.

"More than okay." She smiles and hugs him tightly.

"Good," he says before flopping to the floor and picking at his pajama feet. Frankie watches him with a smile on her face. Her right hand nervously fumbles with a ring on her left hand—a simple ring her father gave her for finishing her doctorate degree. I'm sure her father hates me now more than he did before. No one is ever good enough for your child, no matter how wonderful they might be.

"I'm going to shower," Frankie says. She reaches down and messes up Chase's hair before walking down the hallway.

Chase watches her go before fixing his hair as best as a seven-year-old can. He climbs into her abandoned chair, his legs straight out since he's not tall enough for it yet. He stares at the hallway, and I can tell he wants to say something but is waiting for the right time. The sound of the shower fills the room, and he looks right at me.

"I really like her," he says with a serious expression on his face.

"I'm glad," I answer, unsure of the context.

"Does it bother you I called her my aunt?" he asks, still very serious.

"Not really. I had plenty of aunts and uncles growing up. They weren't blood relatives either, so no, it doesn't," I answer as honestly as possible.

"She's bad at video games. Couldn't even handle controlling the race-car, and I gave her the steering wheel controller." He laughs and brings his legs in to sit Indian style.

"I'm surprised she played games with you." I look down at the table, my eyes scanning the various pages.

"Why?"

"I couldn't get her to play anything during our entire relationship. She used to argue that she was a Nintendo player. Anything more than two buttons would be too much. I bought the old games on Xbox and she still refused to play," I say, never looking up at him.

"Well, she is horrible," Chase says as if that explains everything. "I tried to teach her, but she kept hitting the wrong button to fire. I don't think a trigger is that hard, right?" Chase sighs with exasperation.

"Kiddo, some dogs just can't be taught new tricks unless they want to learn. She's not like us," I answer simply.

"She fell asleep on the couch during the main alien battles. I needed help fighting them off, but she was snoring! Who does that, Aunt Jazzie?" Chase says with his hands waving around for emphasis.

"Apparently, your other aunt does. What time did you manage to crawl into bed?" I hear my mother's voice coming out of my mouth.

"I had to get Aunt Frankie to wake up, down the hall, and into bed before I could go to my room." He fidgets in the chair. My mom used to say my brother did that when he was fibbing. She told me children are innocent so they tell fibs, but adults lie because they are old enough to know better. It's a cute way of looking at things, but in the end a lie is a lie.

"What time did you actually get to bed?" I ask, my full attention on him as I lean back on the couch. He looks at me and then to his feet.

"Just told you," he says softly.

"No, you said you went to bed after helping out your aunt. You never gave me a specific time." I take a deep breath and try to prevent my mother's voice from coming out of my mouth again. "Just tell me the truth; no harm, no foul. Okay?"

"I waited for you to check up on me," he says to his feet. "I needed to make sure you were home okay. Didn't want to wake up and . . ." He trails off.

I wave my hand and he quickly rushes to my side, his little arms wrapping around me as tight as they can. It still amazes me how he can go from laughing to borderline tears in seconds. Frankie said he'd grow out of that in time as he gets different experiences. She doubted the fear of being abandoned would ever go away, but it wouldn't control him as much.

"I'm sorry about that. I had to check on something before I came home. I wasn't too late though, right?" He nods against my chest. "How about you call me whenever you need, okay? Even if it's pretty late. That way you know I'm okay and you can sleep."

"You should have slept in your own room," he says to my stomach.

"Chase, Frankie and I . . ."

"Aunt Frankie," he says, correcting me.

"Aunt Frankie was sleeping, and I didn't want to wake her up." I hope my explanation will be accepted. It's much more than that, but he's too young to understand any of it. He slowly lets go of me and leans back with his arms crossed. His face holds an expression I can't quite place.

"You love her." He nods defiantly. My brother did that all the time when he was being serious. Even into his late thirties, it was his trademark. When he had a point, it was arms crossed, say the line, and nod. As if that was the end of the discussion, and I wasn't about to reply. It stopped working on me when I was fifteen, but he kept trying.

"Chase, I know you think you know everything, being seven and all, but I don't know what you're talking about." This is a conversation Frankie and I need to have at some point. I don't want to start an emotional roller coaster with the kid first.

"Aunt Jazz," he says, uncrossing his arms and taking my hand in his smaller ones, "I love you very much, but you don't see what's right there. Like in Halo when the alien drops a better weapon. You just run over it. You gotta pick it up, Aunt Jazz." In his own roundabout video gamer way, he makes sense to me.

"First off, I run past those guns because they overheat too fast. Secondly, I'm supposed to listen to a young boy wearing long pj's with attached feet?" I pull his legs toward me and start tickling him to lighten the mood. He slaps my arms away as he fights laughing too loud.

"Did you lose her because of me?" he asks, and just like that all the playfulness is gone. "Is that why you cry at night?" His eyes well up a bit, and I realize this conversation has been a long time in the making. With or without my desire to have it, this kid needs some closure now.

"Nothing is because of you." I let him sit back up and keep my distance. He needs answers, not touchy-feely bullshit.

"I showed up and then a little while later she moved out, even before the court stuff was done," he forces out, his hands clenching into fists.

"That's true, she did, but it wasn't because of you, honey." I grab his little fists and hold them tightly in my hands. "She left because of me. When your daddy died, I got really lost and I had to figure out a way to take care of you. Gosh, Aunt Frankie was so good to you and loved you the minute you were born. Did you know that?" I ask as my emotions start to get the better of me.

"No." His reply low and muffled.

"She used to hold you at night to calm you down when you couldn't sleep. When I could barely . . ." I take a deep breath and try to calm myself back down. "When I could barely deal with anything in the world, she loved you. She helped me with all the things for your parents and court papers. She was nothing but amazing," I finish.

"Then why'd she leave us?" he whimpers.

"Because I handled everything so badly. She tried to help me through it, and I pushed her away. I was mean, cold, and everything you shouldn't be to the one you love. I let her down and broke her heart. In turn, she broke yours, and I'm so sorry for that, buddy."

I wait for him to say something in response, but he just sits there calmly. The shower is still going down the hall, and I'm thankful Frankie takes forever in the bathroom. I feel his fists unclench as he pulls his hands away from mine. He puts them on either side of my face and looks at me as seriously as his father did the day he died.

"She still loves you." It was so sincere it almost pulls a sob from deep inside my chest.

"Oh, honey, how do you know that? Love isn't something you can just turn on when you think the time's right. It's more complex than that. So much has happened between us that love might not be enough, regardless of how we feel."

"I know Daddy loved Mommy very much. They would fight over silly things, but he said that's what people in love do. They fight but they make up."

"Chase, you were just a—"

"I found Daddy's notebooks. He and Mommy would write to me every night. When Mommy had me in her belly, she told me about how I made her sick and stuff. When I was born, Daddy wrote in it. I also heard you talking to Aunt Frankie a lot about them. They sounded happy, even though they would fight. She's here because she loves us. She wore that silly shirt that makes you feel safe to bed. She's our family, Aunt Jazz. She loves us and we love her. I don't get it."

I fall silent, unsure of what to say to him. My brother and his damn notebooks. I remember when they asked me to write a few things in there for him. I'm sure nothing as personal as his parents, but I wrote some things. He's such a cute little mess of innocence but other times he's a ninety-year-old in a smaller body. I know I love her; that's never wavered for me. Ever.

"Can I go to the park?" he asks quickly.

"I would love to take you, but I have work on this all day. Maybe Aunt Frankie can bring you?" I say, rubbing my eyes gently hoping to remove all the stress and emotion lingering there. My parents used to do that all the time. Between my hand resting on my lower back and my damn eyes, I have officially become my mother. If only my hair would move an inch or so back when I was angry, that would help get the point across to perps.

"She said she was busy." He begins bouncing at the end of the couch, back to a normal kid with way too much energy coiled up inside him. All of those serious conversations he hit me with a few seconds ago, and now he acts like he's had too much sugar.

"Then I guess you get to play video games all day today," I say, turning my attention back to the papers. I'm sure he's upset, but what kid would turn down a full day of alien annihilation. He shuffles closer, and I can feel those pleading eyes staring at me.

"What about the guys following me?" he says.

"What guys?" I ask, genuinely concerned.

"The two guys in black suits that were at school yesterday? The ones sitting in the black car that followed me and Aunt Frankie home?" He holds his hands up like he's Captain Obvious. He grabs a gruesome crime scene photo from the table and holds it up. "Are they keeping me safe from the man who did this?"

"Chase, stop." I grab the photo out of his hand and try to wash the image of his mutilated body from my mind.

"Tell me the truth."

"Fine," I say to shut him up. "Yes, they are there to keep you safe. No one's going to hurt you, but with this case . . . I need to know you're okay at all times," I finish, omitting some minor details.

"They're really nice guys." He smiles at my shocked expression. "Hank's a really good gamer, but Tim isn't into it. He tries, but Hank says he would make Aunt Frankie look like a champion. That's really sad if you think about it. I mean he shoots a gun, and he can't kill zombies." Chase shakes his head.

"You've met them?"

"They were watching me at recess. I went to say hi, and we talked about the games in this month's magazine you get."

"Right, of course." Leave it to Chase to find a way around a precautionary protective detail that's supposed to be hidden.

"So, can they take me to the park?"

"Sure, if they want," I concede. He's already made friends. What's the harm?

"Okay." He hops up and rushes out the front door, tossing caution to the wind. I jump up and run to the front door as I see the kid safely in the backseat of our security's unmarked sedan. After watching him leave from the front windows, I curl up into a ball on the gray couch in the corner. When I was five or six, I used to sleep on this thing at my grandmother's house; it was better than any bed she had. But once I hit five feet plus, it wasn't so comfortable anymore. If I close my eyes really tight, I swear I can still smell her perfume on the leather.

"You okay?" Frankie asks me, and I feel her hand running up and down my arm.

"Yeah, just tired," I say, unmoving.

"You want a fresh cup?" she asks, and I simply nod in response. I can hear her walking around the kitchen, but I'm more focused on the smell of the leather. I hear the mug hit the table and a familiar smell fills my nostrils—the CK One that she loves to put on after a shower and gives me sneezing fits.

"Are you going to look at me?"

"That depends."

"On what?"

"On if you're going to yell at me for kissing you," I answer simply. "I'm sorry if I put you in a bad position, but I don't regret it. I never will." I open my eyes and see the turmoil in hers. "I'm going to take a shower. Be back in a few." I stand up and turn to walk away, but Frankie grabs my hand and stops me.

"I'm sorry I left you. It was the hardest thing I've ever done, and I regret it every day." Her voice barely registers above a whisper, but I hear it. She lets go of my arm, and I walk down the hallway.

Standing in the bathroom with a locked door behind me and overly bright Hollywood bulbs illuminating my face, silent tears roll down my cheeks. Everything I've lost, everything I am, is written on the lines etched into my skin. All the changes in eye color, skin tone, and every gray hair are a timeline for the person I've become. Looking at my reflection in the mirror, I find I don't like her very much.

In the shower, I turn the dial to the hottest setting my skin can tolerate. The steam rises quickly, filling the room in a fog similar to what's happening in my mind. My hands turn from a pasty white to red as the temperature gets hotter with each passing second. My tears stop with the pain that radiates through my body as the water gets too hot. Turning it down, it clicks that this is just an easier form of self-harming. No scars if you time it just right. Not smart or safe to do either, and that sours my mood even more.

"You've got to focus on what is right in front of you, dammit," I say to the action figures Chase uses in his nightly bath. All of my psychology classes back in the day spouted the importance of speaking things out loud. Sometimes it makes you accept what's going on in front of you. I do it because when I talk to myself, I can usually visualize the puzzle better. Either way, most psychologists just want you to talk. That way they can medicate you, get their kickbacks, and ensure you'll be a patient for a long time. Frankie's not one of them. She hates medication and only uses it if absolutely necessary.

"Three dead bodies and they all look somewhat similar." I grab the kid's pink bar of soap. "First victim, strangled from behind. Simple and easy kill. Nothing fancy about the scene or the dump. This couldn't have been their first one or there would have been more hesitation. So, either the others came before this one, or the perp's been doing this for a while somewhere off my radar."

Rinsing off and grabbing the shampoo, I find myself singing a random song badly. My voice echoes off the floor-to-ceiling tile in the bathroom. The third victim had to mean something more. There was a lot of anger. No blood at the scene, so it was an obvious dump. "What caused that kind of response? Did she fight back harder than the others? Did she make more noise or disobey them?"

That little bit of information could help Frankie build a more in-depth profile. This guy chooses his ladies carefully, right down to the smallest physical detail. This latest victim was different. Maybe something triggered them or maybe have some darker hidden meaning. Either way, any little bit of information I can get helps. I once solved a murder due to a peanut allergy. Everything and anything is relevant. Except when it rains. Then nothing is worth a fucking damn. It all washes away down the drain, like victim two.

"Maybe the perp just hates when their plan goes awry, and there's nothing more important than that. Hell, who doesn't hate when their well thought out plans go to waste. I sure as hell do." My head comes to a full stop. My body shrinks down to the base of the shower, knees pulled firmly into my chest.

Flashes of memories fly by as I try to control the anxiety attack that has taken control. Frankie's voice as she was packing up her last box to leave. Telling me I had new responsibilities, and I apparently didn't want her help. How I shut her out and she wasn't Chase's guardian. I had to learn how to deal with this on my own; she couldn't do it for me. And other things. She had her reasons for leaving, but none of them felt real to me.

It was all whispers on the wind, like promises to be there for you when you grow up. Like those before her that held my heart, she abandoned me. Maybe there's more to her reasoning, and I should have asked her, but I never have.

My mind rolls to the other women I've seen Frankie with lately. Maybe that's why the kiss in my office was such an unwelcomed one. She might just be friends with those people, but my jealousy of them burns close to hatred. Without thinking of the consequences, my left arm swings and my fist connects with the wall. Silent sobs as my body shakes, allowing the anxiety to better me. The knots in my neck and back scream as they tighten in response.

There are so many crossroads we come across during our lives that I can't even remember where they were. So many decisions, so little responses, and somehow we have to assume we made the right choices. Right now, I feel like I'm looking at one path that's dark and dreary and another that's completely unseen, with no information about either one to assist me in making a proper choice.

"Make a wrong choice and more people die. Make the right one and maybe you die," I mumble, finally finding my voice.

My mother always called me a pessimist. My father told me to stop looking at the darker side of life as there is more beauty out there. My brother called me a drama queen. I prefer to think of myself as a realist. In this line of work, when you study people constantly, all you see is the negative. You can try to twist it whatever way you like, but the darkness lurks like cancer within every human body. We face death every day without ever knowing it. That's realism. So, in my case right now, I can't make a choice about which path to choose. I can't walk away because it's not just me anymore. I have to put Chase's safety before everyone else. Period.

Forcing myself to stand up, finish the shower, and towel off, I tiptoe into my bedroom. A small smile spreads across my face when I see clothes laid out for me just like she used to when I was stressed. She didn't do it all the time, but when I was particularly out of sorts on a case, Frankie would lay my outfit on the bed. Made me think of her all day just by looking at my reflection.

"You okay, Aunt Jazz?" I hear Chase through the door. That was a short trip to the park.

"Yeah, just give me a second," I say as I start getting dressed.

"You were in there a long time," he continues. "Did you play with my toys again? They're not for adults you know."

"No sweetie, those are yours." I finish getting dressed and open the door. "I thought you were at to the park with Tom and Hank?"

"I was, but I forgot my lucky sweatshirt and I wanted to say goodbye to you." He wraps his arms around my waist and squeezes tightly. "You going to be okay without me?"

"I think I can manage." I laugh at his protectiveness.

"You sure? Aunt Frankie made a few phone calls and said something about needing backup. I don't really get it," he says, letting go of me.

"Oh boy. That means your Aunt Frankie is up to something and needed Hadley and Victor to help her with it."

"That's not good," he replies with a smile on his face. "Let's go."

Chase walks a few steps in front of me, his back firmly planted against the wall. I walk normally behind him, and he stops when I make the floor creak. He turns back, shakes his head, and points to the wall. I lean against it and follow his lead. We get to the end of the hallway, and muffled voices hit our ears. He takes a peek into the room and stops me from moving.

"The living room's been invaded." He smiles at me. "I don't think we can get pass them."

"How many? Did the bad aliens leave any weapons on the floor?" I continue his game.

"Nope. You wouldn't pick them up anyway." He tries to hide his laughter. "Two girls, a tall guy in a suit. Could be pod people, or zombies."

"That's not too bad. I think we can take them." I rub my hands together, trying to channel my best GI Jane impression. I push off the wall slightly, but Chase places his hand on my stomach.

"Daddy always said girls are the ones who give you gray hair and make your wallets empty. We can take the guy easily, but we have to be very careful."

"Well, I don't have anything in my wallet, and I don't have gray hair."

"We've been over this before. Your wallet's empty because you paid someone to make the gray go away. This is serious, Aunt Jazz. I have to make it to the boys outside of the house. I can't be gray at my age," he says seriously, and I smile at him.

"Well then, I think I have a plan," I say softly as I lay down on my stomach so I have a low profile.

"I'm listening," he says in the most adult voice possible given his age as he joins me on the floor. We crawl to the entrance.

"Okay, I'm going to hit that mark at nine o'clock. I'll create a serious diversion, and you hit the mark over there at one o'clock and then out the door. Just make sure to use the furniture as cover. You miss one spot . . . it might be over. I don't have the power to take them all on myself," I say, pointing to various things in the room. Chase looks like I just gave him some word problem about two people on a train. "You run as fast as you can to your cop buddies outside while I keep the pod people busy."

"Okay, you sacrifice yourself so I can play. I won't forget this," Chase says as he crawls to hide behind the couch. I stand up, nod to him, and walk into the room.

"Frankie, what's going on here?" I shout in an overly dramatic way.

"I thought you could use a fresh set of eyes on the case," she says, lifting one eyebrow at my antics.

I wave my hand in Chase's direction, and he shimmies from the couch to a chair. He tries to stay hidden, but it's terribly obvious where he is. They all look at me, and I simply shake my head in response, waving my right hand for them to keep talking.

"Yes, we all wanted to help." Hadley replies, smiling at me. She deliberately turns away from the furniture so her back is to the front door. Chase rushes out from behind her and stops at the front door. He gives me a thumbs-up before rushing away to freedom.

"It took you thirty minutes to shower and get changed."

"Sorry, Victor, next time I'll just hose myself down and wear a potato sack."

"Maybe next time you shouldn't try to figure out the case in the shower while talking out loud to yourself," Hadley interjects.

"I did no such thing."

"Umm, yes you did." She smirks.

"Hadley, how would you know?"

"Because I had to pee and you were hogging the bathroom. I was going to knock, but you were busy talking to yourself about a lot of things. So, I thought it was best to leave you alone."

Privacy is such a thing of the past. So are my tactics to help my mind break down a case.

"Jazz, your ears are red," Hadley pipes up again. Sometimes, I really want to smack her.

"My ears are not red, Hadley," I answer defensively.

"Yes, they are. Which means you're embarrassed at your little habit." Victor smugly smiles at me.

"My dear Victor, my habit isn't as bad as eating near corpses," I sputter out like a little sister trying to get Mom to punish my big brother.

"Hey, we've been through this, and the bodies don't mind." He raises his voice in his defense.

"You eat around dead bodies?" Hadley questions Victor, her voice filled with disgust.

"What's wrong with eating in my office?" Victor sizes Hadley up as if ready to fight.

"Because you work in the morgue!" She folds her arms across her chest as if that would get her point across faster.

"Do you eat with zombies in full makeup?"

"That is so different," Hadley stammers, a bit offended.

I watch the two banter back and forth, but the sound of laughter pulls my attention to Frankie, who's sitting on the couch, her arm wrapped around her stomach with tears forming in her eyes. It's a rich sound I haven't heard in a really long time. Her face might show all the stress that life has given her, but right now she looks as youthful as ever.

"Come on, eating with fake dead people in costume is not the same as eating with a really dead person," Hadley screeches, waving her hands waving.

"You're right, because the real dead don't reek of bad corn syrup and sweat under the prosthetics. Not to mention, they don't talk back or have bad breath or want your autograph!" Victor says with what sounds like jealousy in his voice, his arms crossed, and a bounce back and forth from left to right.

"No, they just smell like those toxic chemicals you use on them." Hadley's in full defense mode. When she starts to feel like someone is questioning her ability as an actress, she goes all out to fight back. Sometimes that can be painful as it involves full arm waving, then they cross or go to her hip when listening, and back to waving when talking. All of this is topped with lots of high-pitched monologues.

"What the hell are you talking about?" Victor says, confusion etched on his face.

"That crap that turns your insides into mush before you suck it out our noses! That's not what I want to see when I'm eating my sushi. It also sucks for the environment and Mother Nature in the end," she answers back as Victor ducks a swinging right arm.

"We call that embalming. You know that's to prevent decomposition, right? So people can have time to say goodbye," he says much more calmly than his previous statements. Hadley holds firm, hands on her hips as she considers her next statement.

"Your ears are still red," Frankie whispers standing next to me.

"Hot shower," I say.

"That line would work on any number of people in the room. Me, not so much," she replies with a smirk.

"I know, but it's all you're going to get out of me right now," I say, allowing some flirtation to enter my voice. Her cheeks turn a bit red in response, but she says nothing.

"I do not embalm people, Hadley. I do autopsies. I cut people open and try to find the cause of death," Victor says.

"Exactly, cutting people up, taking out the organs, and acting like a mad scientist," she replies defiantly.

"Yes, in an odd sort of way, I guess so."

"Then you can easily liquefy people too."

Victor's mouth falls open and he waves his hands around as if trying to show no connection between the two. Hadley stands there smiling, and part of me wonders if she's just pushing his buttons for fun at this point.

"You're ignoring me," Frankie whispers again so close to my ear I can feel her breath.

"I don't know what you're talking about." I try to keep my breathing calm and focus on ignoring how close she is to me.

"I've got years of experience with those ears. Trust me." Her hand brushes the hair away from my right ear, and I turn my head to face her. Her hand falls on my cheek and her thumb traces the line of my cheekbone. It's something she's done a million times before, but this time it means so much more to me. I lean into her hand, close my eyes, and concede defeat of the subject.

"I'll get you some fresh coffee." She pulls her hand away and leaves me standing there. It's then that I notice the silence in the room. Looking over to Victor and Hadley, my ears start to burn as if they're on fire. The two of them stare at me, waiting for an explanation, I'm sure, but I don't have one.

"Had, Victor does not liquefy people." Victor nods and points to me. "He's had a body that was so badly decomposed it was a pile of goo on his table, but that wasn't his fault."

"Seriously, Jasmine, stop while you're ahead," Victor says.

"Either way, he shouldn't be eating around those bodies. Who knows how many medical codes you're violating on a daily basis down there," Frankie says, handing me a mug. "You know better than to expose evidence to that kind of cross contamination."

"See, you shouldn't eat around death." Hadley throws one final jab at Victor who at this point just takes it in stride.

"Frankie said you were stuck with this case. Can we focus on that please?" he says.

Frankie and I sit on the couch with Hadley and Victor sitting across from us in the two chairs. Leaning forward, I organize the piles in the proper order before attacking the situation. I grab the first picture and hold it up.

"First victim, strangled like the others. Not much at the scene. Everything was very clean," I say.

"Body showed no signs of defensive wounds. I thought there might have been some drugs involved, but nothing came up in her bloodwork. No hesitation marks, no hairs or fibers. Literally, this woman was cleaned up," Victor says.

"That's highly unusual," Frankie adds. "Most assailants take a few tries before getting the killing down just right. They need time to perfect their techniques."

"So, it's possible we have someone who's flown under our radar and we've never found the bodies," I reply.

"It would fit the profile. He's methodical, he studies his victims, knows the area . . . It's out of character to leave his hunting grounds like that," Frankie says convincingly.

"If he's been able to dispose of the test bodies, why not these?" Hadley asks a really good question.

"Trophies? Embarrassment? Could be any number of things, I guess. Second victim, Riverside Park, rain washed away all the evidence from the scene." I hold up the second photo.

Victor gives all the information he has. "Second Jane Doe, no evidence of animal predation or swelling. She wasn't in the water or the park for that long. Someone waited for the perfect time to dump her body. Again, a natural blonde, hazel eyes, all the characteristics of the victim before her. Beyond that, nothing stands out."

"Seems like he's awfully specific about his victims." Hadley whispers.

"That would make sense, but it also limits his pool of candidates," Frankie replies. "That means he takes his time. He has to find someone that fits his desire, and then plan an attack. That is rather intense and detailed."

"Not to mention the bodies are dumped in specific places that are either difficult to pull evidence from or the weather washes it away," Victor adds.

"Final victim, another dump job, scene released due to connections to the city, and from the images, it looked like horrible. Considering the wounds, you would expect blood everywhere, but nothing was noted," I say, summarizing the last file I have.

"It was a brutal attack. Defensive wounds were present all over the body. I found a small wood shard in the right arm, but that could have been connected to anything laying around in the basement. She was sliced, torn up, and tossed out with the garbage," Victor finishes.

"What else do you have? Maybe we can come up with other starting points," Hadley says.

Flipping open the first file, I grab some crime scene photos and spread them out.

"I've got some lovely photos of a useless crime scene and some of the victim. As Victor already pointed out, all three victims were strangled to death," I say, looking over the spread of images.

"You know that's a very personal way to kill someone." Frankie reaches for the first photo on the table. "Do you know what the murder weapon was?"

"Truthfully, the bruising was a bit abnormal. Due to the delay in getting the bodies, environment, and other factors out of my control, I can't pinpoint it. Some bruising could be from fingers, but mostly it looks like a foreign object," Victor says as he tosses a different photo back on the pile. "I wish I could narrow it down, but it's been annoyingly inconclusive."

"Not to sound harsh, but does it really matter how personal something is? Killers get some kind of enjoyment from their actions. Simple. The manner of death is the least of my concerns. This guy wants to eliminate people; that's all I really care about," I say to the room.

"And that's why you're the detective and I'm the psychologist," Frankie says in full-out doctor mode. "Shootings can be vague. Some depend on what weapon was used or the distance from the actual target. Personally, I look at those on a case-by-case basis. Each one is very different from the one before it, but strangling someone never changes. There's a rage that's built over a period of time that manifests itself in consciously closing the path of oxygen to someone's brain. You can hear the person struggling, gasping for life. They fight you constantly as they try to free themselves from death. To me, the only difference is whether the assailant attacked from the front or behind. The rest is the same."

"Thanks for the psychology lesson, doctor, but as we've already discussed, there was only one victim with defensive wounds. That indicates the person knew their killer and allowed him access." I hand Frankie the medical reports. She scans each one briefly as Hadley and Victor have a private conversation between the two of them.

"You two want to share with the rest of the class?" I throw out angrily.

"Hadley was curious about the bruise pattern. It was slightly cylindrical, but awkward at the bottom. Not enough to be a baseball bat, but I surmise it's something similar. Even if we were sure about what it might be, I still couldn't say conclusively it was the murder weapon," Victor says.

"It was a mistake." Frankie tosses the files back on the table before she stands and begins pacing. "The other women were surprised by their attacker from behind, leaving them little time, if any, to fight back before they lost consciousness. The last victim was more fit than the others. If she landed a blow or two, it could be enough to set them off."

"Which explains the vicious attacks postmortem, but I'm at a loss at the connection between all the victims," Victor states as he flips through more photos that Frankie has left behind as she paces back and forth. Victor stops suddenly, three photos sprawled out in from of him. "He stalked them."

"We know he chose his victims carefully, down to their physical attributes. How could he not know the last victim was stronger? They have more muscle definition that's obvious to the human eye. Why go after her?" I say, watching Frankie continue to move around the room.

"Maybe their original target slipped out of their grasp?" Victor says.

"It's possible. All that hard work and research tossed away would create an intense response," Frankie adds.

"That's all plausible, but there's no evidence to back it up," I add. Hadley sits in her chair, looking like she wants to throw up, her face pale, her eyes locked on the pictures of the three victims in her lap.

"Had, you okay?"

"Yeah, sure, fine." Her eyes never leave the photos in front of her.

"Look, we know he watches them. How does he find out about them in more detail? Does he dig through their mail? Hack their emails?" Victor says, playing with his hair.

Hadley places the photos back on the table, stands up, and moves to the other side of the room.

"Hadley, what's going on? You look like you're about to be sick," Frankie says, pulling the attention from everyone in the room. I watch our psychologist trying to analyze Hadley's movements. It's not an easy task to do. Our friend is an amazing actress, and she really only lets you see what she wants you to see. Everything else is locked away.

"It's probably nothing." She tries to instill calm in the room, but the fear is rolling off her in buckets.

"It's obviously something to you, so talk," I say as I stand up and walk around the chairs closer to her.

"I don't even know if it's relevant. It just popped into my head, and I don't know why I didn't think about it before. Hell, you're all probably thinking, 'there goes the dumb actress who's only good for some sex or full-frontal nudity scene before her death.'"

Victor stands up and grabs Hadley's hands. She stares at him, and he speaks so softly I can't make out what he's saying. She nods, takes a few deep breaths, and closes her eyes. She opens them a few seconds later and stands behind Victor.

"He used his forearm." Hadley wraps her arm around Victor's throat and squeezes gently. Victor smirks as he sidesteps before tossing Hadley over his shoulder and onto the floor.

"But anyone trained in self-defense would know how to handle the attack. Whereas if the woman was smaller in stature, she'd be an easier target. The bruising on the third victim would be make sense if they were facing one another. The perpetrator had to deviate from his normal routine," I say. The puzzle is starting to come together.

"And deviating made him angry, and he took it out on the victim's body," Frankie interjects.

"Okay, we have a plausible explanation for everything, but . . ." I let the last word hang in the air as I take a closer look to all the photos.

"They all look like me," Hadley throws out to the group as if it was a simple statement. "Same height, hair, and eye color. Maybe I did something wrong?"

Frankie immediately pulls Hadley into a hug for support. "Sweetie, just because the killer has a type doesn't mean you're responsible for any of it. You're an actress; you know women who look similar to you are a dime a dozen. We don't know enough about this case right now to make any solid judgements." Hadley pushes away from Frankie. "The hardest part of helping out here is seeing things objectively. We have nothing connecting you to the case. Yes, we all see they look like you, but beyond that there's no physical evidence of anything else."

Hadley says nothing as she moves to my dust-laden movie collection in the corner. She grabs one and pops it into the Blu-ray player. After she turns everything else on, I see the title card for her film, *Psycho Zombie Ninja,* on the screen. The three of us are silent as she flips through the chapters.

"It's a love story at heart. The girl rejects this guy who goes to a bar and gets wasted and bit by a zombie bartender. So he becomes part of the undead living among us, all the while being trained to be a ninja to fight the war with the living." She clicks on a specific point and watches a few seconds before fast-forwarding a bit. Once she reaches her scene, she pauses the film on her face and turns to face us. "He uses a camera to find his perfect victim. Once he does, he uses his ninja skills to go undetected. He gets into position, rushes the victim, lifts them off their feet, and strangles them with his forearm from behind." She hits play, and we all watch as Hadley's character dies in the film exactly as we assume the victims have in real life.

"Hadley, this could mean any number of things." Frankie says, trying to diffuse the situation.

"It wouldn't explain the conversations I had with Mr. Murderer over the phone or the threat to Chase," I add, hoping that this little bit of information will get Hadley to calm down.

Hadley shakes her head at the three of us and marches across the room. She grabs the crime scene photos and throws one in front of us.

"Old warehouse." She throws another one. "The pier."

Before she can continue, Victor grabs the photos from her.

"We know where the bodies were dumped. Calm down a second and think about what you're actually saying," Victor says to an obviously shaken Hadley.

"Filming locations," I say mostly to myself. Adrenaline pumps through my body as my face flushes red. "I had to drive you to all of those locations because your car broke down."

"How many locations are we talking about here?" Frankie chimes in, her voice drenched with concern.

"A lot. It was an independent film with a lot of guerrilla shooting. They would find something that morning and we'd be there that night. If we were caught, we had to find a different place. Nothing was ever set in stone or legal," Hadley answered.

"For all we know he's been dumping bodies all over those locations. He could be into the double digits by now," Victor says, dumbfounded.

"Do you remember all of them?" I ask Hadley.

"No, most fell through the moment we got there. It was so long ago; I just remember where we shot the bigger sequences," she answers.

"How does all this relate to my phone call?"

"In the film, the killer hunts and murders all these women as if he's in training. His ultimate goal is to kill the original girl who hurt him. He stalks her, calls her, and watches her all the time. Everyone who dies before is just to get to the main course." Hadley turns the movie off and shuts down the system before looking directly at me. "You drove me to all the locations. You're always my bodyguard at horror conventions. Everyone who cares to look online can find out that you're one of my best friends. If they're training to kill someone—namely me—who else would you choose to hurt first?"

"Take out the bodyguard and get instant, direct access to the prize," I say as bile rises up my throat. This case just went from confusing to sincerely fucked-up. Everyone in this room just became a potential victim, and that means Chase is in the line of fire as well.

"What's going on in that head of yours?" Frankie asks me as she takes my hand in hers. I'm sure she can smell the worry rolling off my skin. Her thumb rubs the back of my hand. I kiss her knuckles before walking into the kitchen away from the group.

I wait a few seconds to make sure no one else is coming in here before pulling out my cell phone. I dial the one man I know I can trust.

"Is there a reason you're calling my personal line?" Captain Udall chirps through the receiver at me.

"My apologies sir, but this is important." I can hear him lean back in that old leather chair by his desk.

"I'm listening."

"I need protection for Victor, Hadley, and Frankie," I blurt out as quickly as possible.

"Mind giving me a reason why?" I swear he's calculating the cost in his head.

"Some new information has come to light." The silence on the other end forces me to continue. "All the victims appear to not only look like Hadley, but the method of killing and the locations seem to be connected to a film she was in. Now this could all be just a coincidence, but I'd like to make sure."

"And you think Victor and Frankie are in danger because of their relationship to Hadley? Am I getting this right?" The clink of a glass hitting the wood of his desk echoes through the phone, then the squeal of a drawer opening, then the twist of a bottle top, and finally the sound of the pouring.

"No ice?"

"Not this time." I half expected a hint of a laugh, but he's far too serious right now to enjoy any bit of humor. The captain is all business in situations like this. He always gets fatherly, protective, and by the book. I get nervous, make stupid jokes, and then become defensive and shut down. If we were in the field, the two of us would be pure cop. No room for any other emotions when your gun is in your hand ready to fire.

The current silence on the other end of the line unnerves me right now. I can hear him breathing, plotting, thinking. He's known me for years and understands what I will and won't do when it comes to my family. I hear the glass touch down on the table and the telltale sign of it being refilled.

"Jasmine, please consider what I'm offering here. If this individual is after each of you, it's safer if we protect you in one of our estates. I understand you would prefer to handle this a different way, but right now I think it would be easier to keep an eye on all of you collectively," he says slowly.

"You mean in one of our luxurious roach motels that we call a safe house?"

"Jasmine, they're not that bad." I hear the glass hit the table again, and I understand he's drinking a bit faster than he usually does.

"I don't think we have enough information on this case to force us all into a one room situation. Not yet." I plead with him to see it my way right now.

I hear the three of them mumbling out in the living room. My name pops out of their mouths a few times and more hushed tones follow. I'm sure they're grilling Frankie on her little display earlier, but they're not going to like it when I come back out there.

"Have you thought about Chase and how this might be affecting him?" Udall says after a few moments of silence.

"Yes, sir, I have. We've got a protection detail on him all the time. After discussing it with Doctor Ryan, we agree taking him out of school and locking him away is not the best decision at this time. He doesn't need the added stress. He needs the ability to be a kid the best way he can, given the circumstances," I answer professionally.

I hear the sound of pouring again, which means I've added a dimension to the case he has to think through before answering. I can hear Hadley's voice rising in the outer room as Victor goes on about her rabid fans being freaks of nature. Now I understand why my mother said sometimes she wanted to shut everyone out and run away. I hate silence with a passion, but a little bit of quiet to sort my thoughts wouldn't be so bad.

"Fine, we'll do it your way for now," the captain says calmly. "You'll have round-the-clock protection. No shadowing or hiding in the background, Jasmine. They're going to be in your face, blatantly there. Any of you ditch them, I swear to all that's holy, it will take a dozen or more surgeries to remove your badge from your ass. Are we clear?" he says like a father berating his child.

"Yes, sir. Crystal. One thing though. If said protection gets in my way during the investigation . . ." My voice trails off.

"You'll kick their ass and then ditch them. I know how you operate. I also know a badge has sharp points. Keep cell phones with location active so we can track everyone. Try not to be an asshole to the ones trying to help you, understand?" he finishes.

"Yes, sir." I disconnect the call.

"Maybe if you were more concerned about an actual acting career and not being NUDE in every freaking film you do, we wouldn't be in this mess," Frankie screams as I walk into the room.

Hadley and Frankie stand nose to nose while Victor sits on the couch watching the battle. His head bounces back and forth as if he's watching a tennis match. His legs are pressed tight together, hands folded on his knees. He was part of the discussion earlier, but it's obvious he's been knocked out of it now.

"Ladies. . ." I attempt to get their attention, but my voice barely permeates the room.

"I AM a serious actress! Just because I work in the horror industry doesn't make me any less talented than Angelina Jolie. Who, by the way, has also been naked in films before!" Hadley screams back at Frankie.

"Yeah, when she was doing it to further the storyline, not saying 'Hey, don't forget what you come home to!' That's cheesy, cheap, and frankly makes film feel like a porn." Frankie shakes her head at a stunned Hadley.

"Actually, nudity is quite useful in various ways in film. Gratuitous sex is pointless, but something that makes sense and fits in the storyline is fine, in my humble opinion." The two women look at me like I have ten heads.

"Oh, now you're in trouble," Victor says from the safe confines of the couch. Both women turn to me, about to protest, but I raise both my arms to effectively stop them

"I really don't give a shit about nudity in film or what roles Hadley is taking on. It's her career; let her have it."

"Thank you," Hadley says to me.

"Frankie also has a right to be concerned. You said it yourself. You have the ability to hold out for more money. These jobs just pay your bills, but you continue doing them. Even when you're not comfortable doing them. I don't know how or what you're already doing, but you can say no to those films. If you need help, we're here for you," I continue as if Hadley never spoke.

"Exactly. You're more talented than these films ever give you credit for, Had," Frankie says, her tone calmer and more concerned.

"Now that we have all that squared away, there's something you all need to know. Considering how this perp might want to off any one of us, we officially have protective details. They should be here within the hour with their assignments. Before you even try to argue, the captain wanted all of us in a safe house. As in cramped together in a small, confined space. Possibly even an hourly abode where some of Hadley's former co-stars now hold office hours," I finish.

"That was a bit of a low blow, don't you think?" Hadley looks at me before falling back into the couch. Frankie and Victor smile at my words but say nothing.

"Yes, it might have been, but it got your attention, didn't it?" Hadley throws a pillow at my head, which I expertly dodge.

"If this is because of me, I'm sorry. I never thought any of these films would . . . I just . . . I can't control what people do with what they watch." Hadley hangs her head in disgust.

"I told you before, it's not your fault. People see your movies and find an attachment to you regardless of the film. You can't be held accountable for what someone interprets from your work. If that was the case, nothing would ever be written or filmed," Frankie says. "I still think you're so much better than what you're currently doing."

"You're better than an office with no windows and a stuck-up pencil skirt, but who's judging?" Hadley says with a bit of a chuckle.

A calm seems to come over everyone, but Frankie stands suddenly and walks down the hallway. I hear a bedroom door close and look at my other two friends. Hadley motions for me to go after her, so I do.

My bedroom door still hangs slightly ajar, but Chase's is fully closed. Knocking on the door gently before opening it, I see Frankie sitting on the edge of his bed, a frame in her hand. She looks up at me and pats the bed next to her. Without saying another word, I sit down.

"You think he forgives me?" she asks softly.

"I don't know if there's anything to forgive."

Frankie nods her head and continues to look down at the photo in her hands. It's from when Chase was first born in the hospital. She has her arms around me as I hold this tiny little thing, the biggest smile on our faces. That was before our world burned to the ground.

"I remember this picture. We ran home from class just before visiting hours ended," I say.

"You were so terrified to hold him," she whispers.

"So, you wrapped your arms around us both. Always the protector, even then."

She leans forward and places the frame back on his night table. "You remember the baseball game we took him to?"

"Yeah, he ate so much crap that entire day." I smile fondly at the memory.

"I never thought he'd get to sleep."

"He didn't. Was up until three in the morning talking about how he got a baseball, ran the bases, and ate whatever he wanted. Wouldn't shut up."

"Why was it so different when I lived here?" she asks me.

"I ask myself that a lot. I mean, we were always good with Chase whenever we went out. It was like the door was a gateway escape to something that wasn't real. Once we came home, it felt like all the emotions and loss were here. Lingering like moss on the side of a tree," I answer.

"But you were never totally responsible for him," she says simply. "I remember the trip to the zoo two months after the crash. I heard the two of you laugh for the first time in a long time. We could hide away and still be the cool aunts. The minute we came home, we were guardians again."

"Maybe. There was so much more going on around us that I barely remember that trip."

Frankie takes my hand in hers and squeezes tightly before pressing it to the center of her chest.

"Your brother once told me I was good for you. I helped you make decisions before the turn of the century." I laugh slightly as I think about my indecisiveness. "I just wanted to say I'm sorry. I pushed you and didn't have the patience . . ."

"You did. You still do. You were the best thing for me, Frankie, but I can't have you be that anymore. I can't wake up knowing that I'm nothing without you. I have a kid to think about. I have someone else depending on me, and I need to know that I'm enough without anyone else. I have to be able to hold him up when he's down. I can't expect . . . I can't need you to do that for me." The words are out of my mouth before I can stop them.

Frankie nods and puts my hand down in my lap. She stands up, fixes her clothes, and wipes a stray tear from her face. After gathering herself, she looks directly at me, and I can see the pain my words have caused her.

"That's the thing, Jasmine. You never needed me. I always needed you," she says as she walks out of the room and back to the others. I sit there trying to absorb what she just said, trying to understand the words and how my heart breaks.

"The cops are here, so I'll catch you later." Hadley's words pierce my silence.

"Yeah, sure. What about the others?" I ask.

"Victor already left with a very hot young officer. He was rather happy he needed a detail all of the sudden. Frankie split with some officer chick. Might want to keep an eye on that. I figured since the others already left, I'd be nice and let you know. My guy, Officer James Dunkin, said the captain wants a list of production dates, locations, and crap. I'll get the producers to send it to you. Lord knows they'll love the free press all this attention will get. You need me, you know where to reach me." Before I can say anything, she's out the door as quickly as she came in.

Entering the living room, I see a mid-thirties uniformed officer standing by the door, his thumbs tucked neatly in his belt. "You don't have to stand at attention all the time. You could relax a bit." He looks at me nervously before he approaches, his hand outstretched.

"Detective Steele." I shake his hand with the simple greeting.

"Sergeant Will Everts at your service, ma'am," he properly replies. He lets go of my hand and immediately his thumbs return to his belt.

I head into the kitchen with Will a few steps behind me. "Ma'am is my mother. I might act like her on some . . . well, most occasions, but please just call me Jasmine, Jazz, or Steele. While I appreciate you being here to protect my associates, you really don't need to be so nervous around me." He looks at me oddly, and I point to his thumbs. "You put your thumbs in your belt; sometimes it's a sign of nerves."

Will's chiseled shoulders bounce up in down as he laughs, "No, Steele, I used to put my hands on my belt where I had my grenades. It was more nerves there than here. Now, it's just muscle memory."

"What and how long?" I ask.

"Marines, three tours. Home for good now."

"So, I got the big bad Marine. I must have irritated someone." I laugh.

"No, captain just figured no one else would be able to keep up with you or wrangle you in if need be."

I pour the two of us some coffee and place the mug on the table. "You want milk or sugar?"

"No, this is fine, thank you." He drinks some coffee, relaxing a bit.

"So, what do you think of this case thus far?" I ask.

"I think someone is in for a good ass kicking when we find them." I laugh slightly at his honest reply. Leave it to a military man to say it like it is. Before I can give him a witty answer, my cell phone buzzes on the table.

"Steele."

"Ms. Steele?" an unknown female's voice echoes through the phone. "My name is Jane Michaels, and I'm a nurse here at University Hospital." I grab my coffee and take a sip of the now lukewarm fluid.

"How can I help you Ms. Michaels?" I can hear her flipping through some papers as another voice booms in the background over the intercom.

"I'm calling about Chase Steele. You are listed as his next of kin—"

"Is he okay?" I promptly get up and dump my coffee in the sink. Picking up on my actions, Will is right behind me.

"He appears to be okay, but we need your authorization to get X-rays on his arm and other treatment if necessary."

"You do those X-rays, but call me on my cell if anything else is necessary before I get there."

"Chase is in the hospital." I grab my coat and wallet and fumble around looking for my keys. Will dangles his in front of me.

"No offense, detective, but I've driven at high speeds through minefields. City traffic has nothing on that. Besides, you driving was never an option. Wrangler, remember." Will walks out of the house with me hot on his tail.

"Always the funny man, huh?" He just shrugs his shoulders, and we hop in the car. Thankfully, true to his word, we slice through traffic easier than cheesecake, and in minutes I'm standing in the emergency room waiting for assistance.

I tap on the plastic divider and wait for the nurse to look up at me. She slides the glass over, but barely looks up at me.

"I'm sorry to bother you but—"

She cuts me off. "Have you checked in yet?"

"No, I'm looking—"

"Next window." She slides the divider closed before I can get another word in. I stand there waiting for her to look up again. When she does, she points her obnoxiously long French-manicured nails to the woman seated at the next window. I pull my badge out and slam it against the plastic. She looks up again, undeterred, and points again. If I could arrest people for being ill-mannered, I would have to build an island to house them all.

Will taps on the window next to me with a big grin on his face. The woman behind it promptly opens it.

"Hi, we're looking for Chase Steele. He was brought in here earlier, and the doctor is waiting for us."

The woman smiles, pushes a button under her desk, and I can hear the buzzing sound. Will opens the door and we walk in.

"Right this way," the nurse with common courtesy answers, and we follow her down a hallway full of people. Some are more injured than others; some just chilling and waiting to get some help. Either way, it's an uncomfortable walk. I hate hospitals; they reek of death.

"Aunt Jazzie!" Hearing Chase's voice, I pop my head into a small room and see him sitting on a gurney.

"How you doing, little man?" He lifts up his right arm, and I can see his wrist is swollen and bruised. "I tried to beat the monkey bars, but I lost."

The two officers start laughing slightly, but one look from me and they stop dead in their tracks.

"I'm getting a cast in black because it's cool."

The intern walks in with the items needed for his cast. I watch in silence as the two officers joke around with Chase, the three of them acting as if the injury is no big deal. My heart's still in my throat and I need to swallow it back down.

"You okay?" Will asks me, but I'm still too wound up to reply. "You know, when I went on my last deployment, my wife was taking care of my youngest daughter. She'd send me photos all the time, telling me she was such an active kid. I wanted to wrap her up in bubble wrap and protect that kid from the world, you know? That's what we want to do as parents, but we can't. No matter how Chase came into this world, you're his parent, and that fear you're feeling is real. I won't lie and say it gets easier, but he will heal."

"What if I can't protect him from this guy? What if we don't find him in time and I lose Chase?" I say so Chase and the twin dumbasses can't hear me.

"You find him first. There isn't another option," Will says as if it is the simplest thing in the world to do.

"You're philosophical, aren't you?" He smiles at Chase looking over his new cast. "The desert does that to you." He pauses for a second before he continues. "I think we should take him home. You need to be near him tonight. We'll go to Hadley's film shoot tomorrow."

I look over to see the officers arguing over who will use the Sharpie and sign the cast first. I'm sure everyone around him will. I watch Will give the details for the evening to the others. He's my wrangler, and suddenly my heart is sliding back into my chest.

Chapter Five

Will speeds through traffic, no lights or sirens on to warn the drivers around us. Various cars switch lanes or pull over to get out of the way. Others slow down or ignore us completely; neither stops him from driving like it's a Formula One race through back streets.

"If we took my bike, we'd be there already," Will says over the sounds of my stomach saying my coffee might make a return shortly.

"Right, because bile rising in my throat slowly was a downer for you? No one said we have to turn a thirty-minute drive into fifteen minutes," I say, still holding onto the handle on the ceiling for dear life.

"Blame the military. Avoiding obstacles, bombs, and whatever else is part of our training." He slows the car, searching for a parking spot. With a quick spin of the wheel, Will pulls the car onto the curb, perfectly parking it without hitting the streetlamp or divider.

"You realize there are spots down the street, right?" I ask as I open the door, being careful to avoid the brick wall close to the car.

"Yeah, but I need to protect my ride." He shrugs his shoulders as he gets out of the car, laughing at himself. "I always wanted to park like this just once. It's an abandoned industrial area, so no one will care."

"Oh, hell to the no! You can't park there!" We both turn to see a skinny-looking kid with a headset around his neck. "You need to move this monstrosity right away." He waves his hands around, trying to get either of us to move from where we're standing.

I show him my badge and attempt to walk around him. He weakly places his hand on my chest and shows me the clipboard he's holding. "Your plates aren't on the list, so you don't park. I don't care if you're a cop or the president. Not on the list, you don't park."

"Please let Hadley Moreno know that Jasmine Steele is here to see her," I say, swallowing the urge to break the kid's hand.

"Right, because everyone knows her. Like I said, not on the list, not parking. So, before I call the real police, please move your vehicle." He laughs, still holding the list in my face.

Will reaches forward and grabs the walkie-talkie from the kid's waist, disconnecting it from the earpiece.

"What's Hadley Moreno's twenty?" Will says professionally into the receiver.

The line crackles for a few seconds before we hear a muffled, "Who's on this line?" Will smiles and clicks the button.

"This is the police." He looks at the assistant who I think peed in his pants. "Tell Ms. Moreno that Detective Steele is parked and coming on set to see her. Over and out."

Will hands back the walkie-talkie. Shaking, the assistant plugs the headphones back in and clips it on his belt. "Go ahead," he says, and his eyes dart to the two of us. His shoulders sag, he swallows, and then closes his eyes tightly. I wish I knew what the person on the other end was saying to him, but it can't be good.

"If you would please follow me," he says, finally opening his eyes. Turning around, he opens the locked gate and ushers us inside.

We walk through a maze of wall-to-wall trailers, some more expensive than others with slide outs or second levels.

"I thought you said this was a no to barely-there budget film. Looking around this place, it looks more Hollywood than anything," Will says, taking in the surrounding area.

"That's what she said, but I've never visited her before. I was just the driver," I say in awe.

The assistant stops and turns around, looking almost annoyed at our ignorance.

"Ms. Moreno gets a specific trailer and other perks. Someone of her caliber is given what she wants; then you have all the other people who take cuts here and there. Special effects, blood by the gallons—it all adds up. Just so you know, budgets are relative. No one on set discusses the money unless you want to get fired, but if it's lower than a major studio film, we consider it a low to no budget."

"So, what is the budget for this film?" I ask.

"Independent studio head has a wealthy parent, so it's about five million," the assistant says as if that's nothing. Will and I stop in our tracks.

"For a simple slasher film? You figure with that kind of money the special effects would look less fake," I say in a harsh tone.

"Commoners," the assistant mutters as he walks away from me. Will pulls out his cell phone and dials Officer James.

"Commoner? He does realize he is the lowest on the totem pole in the industry, right? If the director needs to pee in something, that kid either finds a cup, gives up his soda, or opens his pocket," I spit out to the kid's back in the distance. Will looks at me with a grotesque look on his face.

"James, what trailer are you in?" Will smiles at me. "Got it, thanks."

Will looks around before heading into the maze of trailers with me close on his tail.

"You going to enlighten me about which trailer?" I say as we take another turn. Will's eyes scan around.

"The one with the big star on it," he says seriously.

"You're kidding, right? There's no number or something we could look for?"

"That's what he said; I didn't ask any questions. How long has Hadley been acting, anyway?"

"Since we were kids," I say, looking at a few other trailers.

"I'm surprised she's doing low-budget horror then. I'd assume she'd be in LA somewhere with a house on the hillside."

"Didn't work out that way. Besides, all of her childhood films were dreamed up by me and acted out by Hadley and Victor. All of it was done with the sole purpose of entertaining our families. Nothing ever saw the light of day," I say, thankful that the internet had yet to exist.

"So, you did little stage productions for your families. That's not really film."

"Will, I might have been born in the eighties, but my family owned a cheap, antiquated camcorder. It didn't record any sound, so we would videotape it to the best of our ability, air it, and do the dialogue while sitting behind our families. We were rather advanced for kids our age," I say in defense of our pathetic attempts to create anything.

"That explains a lot." Will laughs.

I open my mouth to argue, but the truth is it does explain a lot. We were more advanced than the kids of our neighborhood. While everyone else was catching lightning bugs, we were filming silent movies and our parents encouraged us constantly. We had to focus on completing each project, and our parents watched them all, no matter how bad. It's something we're proud of to this day.

"That wasn't a cheap hobby. I can't imagine editing was easy either."

"Yeah, it wasn't. We had chores, and we earned all our money. You have no idea how hard we worked cleaning the garage, washing the cars, anything to earn a quarter here, and maybe if we were lucky, a dollar there. Nothing was ever given to us for free. If we had to borrow money from one of them, we paid it back with interest. Then one of our parents would take us to get the reel of whatever film we could use with the camera, and we shot it. We ended up destroying a lot of it just to learn how to edit. The things we did cut together . . . it wasn't that good."

"You guys were ambitious."

"Maybe. All I know is to this day I despise mowing the lawn. My dad always loved it to be mowed in this angular way so it looked like Yankee Stadium. Annoyed the crap out of me, not only because our lawn was small and mowing at an angle was a bitch, but because I'm a Mets fan. Go figure."

"My kids are like that."

"Like what?"

"Ambitious. They want to do everything, and I try to help them out as much as I can, but money is always tight. Not to mention they want the latest of everything since their friends have the newest gadget. Try telling a young kid they don't have to keep up with the Joneses with the latest iPhone. Nothing sinks in; you just get asked why you hate them so much."

"Not easy today to get a kid to earn the money either."

"Tell me about it," Will says as the two of us look around, sincerely lost.

"Stop reminiscing about the good old days and someone please tell me how I look," Hadley says from the doorway of an expensive-looking double-decker trailer. James holds his hand out and helps her down the few steps to the pavement.

Her hair, with different colored extensions, hangs perfectly over her shoulders. The black leather pants hugging every curve of her body reminds me of her ridiculous squat workout. The bra strains against her tight, low-cut shirt to push her breasts to the sun, and leather boots with at least a five-inch heel make Hadley look like she is six feet tall. She looks like she's ready for a zombie walk or a Halloween party in my opinion.

"You look . . . different," I say finally.

I look over to James or Will for some assistance, but the two of them are eerily quiet. Will's all red in the face with a shy smile and his eyes looking up and down frantically. James just stands there, hands in his pockets and a bit of drool on his lip.

"Thanks, gentlemen. That's just the reaction I was hoping for," she says, giving me a tight hug.

"If your top gets any tighter there, Hadley, we're gonna have a problem." I laugh a bit to break up the tension. "Either that or your tits will blind someone."

"Well, if you pay attention to the fan forums, you would know that I was voted most likely to stop a war with my body." She smiles proudly.

"Does that include the fact you actually started the war by killing someone with your nipples?" I say teasingly.

"Wouldn't you like to know," she says, and instantly she wins the conversation.

"No, nope, I don't want to know. That's like seeing Victor naked. Nope, not ever!" I say as Hadley laughs at me. Outside of a film set, festival, or convention, she's rather reserved. She watches people and enjoys the everyday small moments that go on around her. Once she steps foot beyond those gates, her confidence soars and she shows it. From the time we were ten, we all knew that Hadley was meant to be in film.

"I wasn't offering, Jasmine. God, there wouldn't be enough Patron in Manhattan to deal with that image." Hadley shudders.

"I wonder how many people fight over you at all the conventions."

"Too many to care about. They do their thing, I do mine and go home to an empty hotel room," she says. "Anything to say, boys?"

Hadley turns her attention to the two other officers who stand silent, staring at her. Will finally blinks and punches James in the arm. The younger officer wipes his mouth off and smiles.

"James, maybe we should make sure the perimeter is clear." James backs away slowly, keeping his eyes firmly on Hadley's body. Will finally pulls him, forcing James's body to shift and break contact.

"He's cute," she says, waving to James as he's taken away.

"He's supposed to protect you, not ogle you."

"Ogling might be a good thing."

"Hadley!" I smack her on the arm.

"What? I'm young, single, and tired of all the men in my field. Maybe I should look for someone who isn't acting, writing, or whatever in entertainment. Seriously, Jasmine, I'm tired of an empty bed."

"Like your bed is ever empty. Hadley, you could have anyone in your bed every night. Stop being so dramatic here."

"Why are you always so cynical about everything? It's hard to look like I do and do what I do. Guys want the actress, not the person."

"Why are you always so shallow when it comes to men? Maybe try to find someone who doesn't look so amazingly hot on the red carpet. Maybe date someone who no one would expect. Someone who actually stimulates your brain instead of just the lower region of your body." I toss back sarcastically. "Are you ready to go to set yet?"

"I'm not shallow." Hadley looks at me, her eyes betraying her pain at my comment. "You think I like putting this shit on to look sexy when I feel like I want to scream in pain right now? My feet don't fit into these boots, let alone the fucking heel is too high for me. Sun is baking the leather, and these extensions weigh a freaking ton. When they take them out, I lose a good amount of hair in the process. But hey, this is me always caring about how I appear to the outside world." She starts to walk away.

"Had . . ." I call after her.

"No, you guys always bitch at me like I'm the stupid one, always worried about my looks and never caring about anyone else's feelings. None of you really expect me to help when you want to go over cases. It's like I'm only there because we've been friends forever. Otherwise, none of you would cut me off as much as you do. You know what? Fuck all of you."

"Stop, you know we don't mean it. We invite you because you do have some good ideas, and you know the rest is just teasing," I say weakly, trying to defend our actions.

"Right, you just tease me. Like when you watch one of my earlier indie films and make fun of what chick is going to be naked next. Or when you mute it and create your own dialogue? You guys don't get how hard it is to make it anywhere in this business. I've had to take those shitty roles to even have a resume so I could get bigger auditions. Everything I do, all the classes, the continuous hard work to get me a chance at a major motion picture. I don't ridicule you for all the screwups you made in uniform. In fact, I tried to help you through it," Hadley says, her hands on her hips. "This fucking leather chafes and never breathes. I sweat like a bitch, but I can't complain because if I do, I lose my job. I work my ass off day in and day out just trying to keep up with these trampy size two wenches who aren't afraid to rip off all their clothes and hang their birthday suit out for the world to see. I don't do that shit, okay? Yet, you guys always make fun of me and call everything I do a cheap piece of shit B movie. Not everyone can make it at a higher level of acting, regardless of whether I want to or not. It's not perfect, but I can demand a bigger paycheck. I have people who respect me in the field. I sometimes get a bit part in a made-for-TV film because of all of these slasher flicks. None of you see the bigger picture, so back off."

"Yeah, but—"

"I'm a serious actress! So people call me their Scream Queen and I have a good following. So what? I audition for serious parts all the time and nothing good comes from it. This stuff pays my bills and allows me to keep working. So, no, it isn't my end goal, and no, I really don't like the creepy people who offer to buy me Jimmy Choos if I would just take pictures of my feet in them . . . or those other whack jobs who email me randomly and ask if I really like bondage. You wouldn't believe the amount of people offering me thousands of dollars to just tie them up and have a drink with them. It's sick, and it freaks me the fuck out, okay?" she finishes in a huff.

"People ask you to take photos of your feet?" I say in a very small voice. Everything she's said is accurate, and it's time we start treating her better.

"Out of everything I said, that would of course be the one thing you latch onto. Yes, I have some freaky people out there who scare me with their requests, and you will not mention this to Frankie," Hadley says with a slight smile on her face. I go to answer, but her hand blocks my face. "I know you were thinking it, so don't even try to lie."

"Maybe I was, but she could give us insight into these potential stalkers and if we should take them seriously," I add in my defense. Hadley stops walking and grabs my arm.

"While I appreciate your protectiveness, you could be murdered by a random person on the street just because they want to know what it feels like to kill. I'm not five anymore. I have all of you to thank for my common sense, and I have an officer attached to my hip raising eyebrows everywhere I go. Isn't that good enough?" she says, her eyes pleading for understanding.

I try to add some humor to the conversation. "I thought any press was good press."

"Normally I would agree with you, but when hiring me could possibly lead to an unfinished film because your star was slaughtered, I'm not sure a director would jump on that casting. Sure, if others could come in to finish my part, or if it was mostly done, you could easily edit around my death, but it could be a pain in the ass. Who would really want to take that on? It's not like I'm going to overdose on drugs or something. You know what you're getting into with this detail. James is adorable, and he's doing the best he can to fit in, but he's a huge red flag."

"If I could fix this, I would."

"I know you would, but you really can't. It has to play out the way it does. I just hope you figure out the ending of the script before I have to perform it." She pulls me back into another hug, effectively shutting the entire discussion down.

Our detail catches up to us, and I can tell from both their expressions they aren't happy with us. James stands right beside Hadley, his eyes once again transfixed on her figure. Will clears his throat and points to his watch.

"James, I have to get to set. Detective, remember what I said," she says with a firm tone.

James holds his elbow out, and Hadley slides her arm inside it. The two walk off, and I am stuck thinking long and hard about her comments. She's fully aware of the plausible target perfectly painted on her back, and she's truly afraid. It's clear the situation is something I can't fix or undo. She just needs me to figure it out before she becomes the leading lady in her own death. Considering the lack of material to go on, that's a tall order.

After they're out of sight, I turn on my heels and head back to the car.

"You want to talk about it?" Will asks.

"No."

I manage to tune Will's voice out as I walk faster to the car. I need to process everything going on around us. Something is missing, and I can't put my finger on it. This is not the kind of life anyone should be living. Walking through crowds in Times Square induces panic in people like me because we understand the risks. Any one of those people can kill you and get away with the ensuing migration of freaked-out people. Opening the car door and hopping inside, I wait for Will to get in.

"I need you to take me somewhere."

"Wherever you want to go."

I pull out a worn, laminated card out of my wallet and hand it to him. "Take me there."

"Jasmine." I hear him turning to face me in the leather seat.

"Please, just drive," I say, staring out the windshield.

Will drives slower this time through traffic. I just sit and watch all the people walking by. I wonder how many of them are going to be alive tomorrow. Life is all about percentages and probabilities. If one in five gets cancer, someone in the subway car with you will get it. I wonder if they feel as connected to each other as I feel to them. Watching the lives of mysterious people just reaffirms my faith that we are all one. Colors, religions, genders, and orientations are just part of the cake mix of life. You can either bake something amazing to enjoy or try to take it apart and watch it rot in the fridge. People need to stop fighting each other, but if they did, I'd be out of the job.

Will pulls the car over against the small curb. He reaches to unfasten his belt, but I stop him. This is something I have to face alone. I let myself out of the car and wander over the freshly cut lawn. The blooming flowers' scent lingers in the air and reminds me I'm alive as I sneeze. The marble tombstones of death rise from the grass like growing weeds. They never truly go away; we just ignore them. It's always been amazing to me how beautiful a cemetery is to try to make us all feel better about our ultimate demise. My worst fear, beyond all fears, is being here. Leaving and going into the abyss of nothingness. Not being able to protect the people I love. I don't figure I'll get a long life. In my line of work, fifty is old. I don't want to die. I've seen too much of it already.

My feet land between two ornate stones. My mother fought hard to ensure my father had a beautiful stone. She didn't much care for it but knew she would be under it eventually. She had purchased two plots long ago: one for her and my father, the other for her children. Interesting plan on spending eternity next to loved ones, but they marry and move on. My mother always had a sixth sense. Maybe she knew Henry would be resting next to her before she went away.

My knees hit the grass before I can fight to remain upright. My hand traces over my sister-in-law's name on the stone. It was a fight to get her into a Catholic cemetery with her being an atheist. Money talks, and so did Frankie. She made it happen for Chase. She was his fighter when he needed her. Now, it's my turn, and to do that I have to say goodbye to some things.

"Hey, guys," I mutter. "I know it's been a while, and I should have visited more often. I know I should bring Chase around too, but I'm not sure if he's ready for this yet."

My fingers follow the letters of my brother's name. I feel the tears, but I no longer care if they fall.

"Chase broke his arm. He said it was on the monkey bars, but I'm sure a girl was involved there somewhere. You'd be proud of your son. He's one hell of a young man. Smart. Strong. Reminds me of you every day."

My hands drop to my sides. His name on that stone reminds me of the finality of it all. My big brother, he's really gone. Not on vacation, not away—he's dead. That's why I hate coming here. It reminds me this is real.

"I'm sorry I wasn't there. I'm sorry I didn't force Dad to get healthy by cooking for him all the time . . . sorry I didn't go out with you all that night. Maybe the accident wouldn't have happened if I did. I'm sorry I put myself first. I'm sorry I let you all down. Maybe if I . . ."

A sob escapes my mouth before I can finish my thoughts. The survivor's guilt I've been carrying around for years seems to be finally free to shake my soul to the core.

"I've slipped and called him my son." My voice shakes. "I took him away from you. I made you disappear in one sentence."

Wiping my eyes, I fling the tears into the dirt below.

"But I don't feel guilty about that. I feel guilty for many things, but loving him enough to call him my son? That makes me proud. You wrote in your will you wanted me to take care of Chase and give him the life he deserves. He will never forget you. I won't let that happen, but he's my responsibility now. I can't give him a proper life until I let all of this guilt go. So, forgive me for everything, but I can't be responsible for everything that happened. I have to focus on being someone you'd be proud of."

I stand up, wipe my face one final time, and take a deep breath.

"I love you guys, and I'll try to come back more often, but I have a lot of work to do."

Tilting my head back, I feel the warmth of the sun on my face. Hopefully, Chase is right and the family is watching us. I hope they are proud and approve of what I'm trying to do. Finally feeling free, I know what I have to do, and I know just where to start.

Chapter Six

I 've always been the type of person who visualizes everything in front of them. Regardless of how many pieces of evidence, or lack thereof, one has to look at the overall idea before making any conclusions. The full global picture always tells more than just the weight of its parts. I have a rather large rolling monstrosity known as a dry erase board in my office. One side is always riddled with notes, ramblings, and thoughts on the case at hand. The other side has all the information that's been confirmed: pictures, names, locations, evidence found, and what it all means. I rarely look at this side. I've committed it all to memory. The faces of the ones lost; they're impossible to forget while the case is still unsolved.

"Those things are going to make you high or burn some brain cells. My first grade teacher told me they were very addictive as well," Will says capping the smelly marker.

"No one asked you to snort my marker, Will," I say, staring at the notes, trying to see how they all connect.

"Sure, take away all the fun from my childhood."

"Somehow that seems to explain a bit more about you. Might want to watch it though; can't have the captain hearing about your addiction. He'd have you in rehab and working a desk for the rest of your career."

"You might be right. I'm already on his radar for the detective's exam. Don't need to give him any more ammunition to bug me about it," Will says, looking over the notes in front of him.

"Take the test, get him off your back, and see what happens," I say, rubbing the back of my neck.

"I did." He grabs the red marker and twirls it in his hand. "Passed with a high score; close to yours actually. Now he's bugging me to suit up."

"If that's what you want to do, you do it. It's not rocket science, man; if you're not cut out for it, you find a different department. Pays better and it gets you off the patrol beat."

"True." Will pops open the red marker, places it by his nose, and inhales. "Oh yeah, that hits the spot!" He laughs as he recaps the marker.

"Where the hell did they find you?" I lean back against my desk in slight awe of his cavalier behavior.

"Steele, this is nothing. You should have been on base with me and my boys. The crap we used to pull on each other . . . markers would have been the least of your worries."

"I'd like to meet them someday, swap stories," I say, not really thinking about the words.

His voice lowers. "I wish you could, but they're long gone."

"Shit, I'm sorry to hear that," I say, hoping the sincerity in my voice comes through.

"You know, when you're over there, humor is really what keeps you going. One minute you could be laughing and the next minute killing a kid with a bomb strapped to his chest. Then, I come home and see these horrible things all over again in my own country. We're trained to see disturbing shit, and we're just expected to dismiss it later on. I can't bring that home to my family. I don't want to drink away the images every night. I can't. So, I try to find the silver lining in anything I can. In this case, I have to laugh at the damn dry erase markers and how we are more old school than the newer precincts with PowerPoint presentations and shit," he says sitting next to me on my desk.

"I doubt they would trust me with a computer after my last situation. Opened some attachment that had a virus. Almost shared it with the whole network. Nothing beats classic crime fighting anyway. Tech can only get you so far."

"Exactly. We are behind the curve in every part of law enforcement upgrades, yet we have the highest percentage of solved cases with included prosecution ratio. We find out the truth with physical evidence. It's not perfect, and sometimes we do screw up, but we work damn efficiently. Maybe they think we don't need the new stuff, but you have to laugh that those who don't do as well get all the funding, and those who seem to excel are passed over."

"Well, thanks for putting an even more depressing outlook on everything. What happened to the silver lining? I think you need to Google the meaning of that phrase and come up with new material."

"Hey, the positive take is that we're better at what we do. We don't need gimmicks or some new fancy social media app to get things done. I don't need to explain everything in some emoticon."

"Emoji. No one says emoticon anymore."

"Whatever, we don't need that crap to succeed. We actually talk instead of the lack of attention span these kids seem to have. In my day, the only thing that pulled us away from anything was the ice cream man."

"Ergo why Frankie and I had no desire to have our own tiny people."

I stop at my sudden comment. It was an odd thing for me to say, and I can see it's made Will a bit uncomfortable. He stares blankly, as if thinking of what to say next. He cracks his neck, and I cringe at the sound. Standing, he faces the board and holds out the marker in his right hand.

"Anytime, boss. We got us a crime to solve." He smiles as he writes CATCH BAD GUY on the board. Someone knocks on the door, and Will quickly caps the marker.

"See what sniffing markers can do?" Will smiles, shakes his head, and sticks out his tongue. He grabs the doorknob and pulls it open, almost running into Frankie in the process. She holds her hands up in shock. Will places his hands on either side of her and gracefully moves her one step to his right.

"Ma'am."

"Am I interrupting anything?" she asks as Will lets his arms fall back to his belt.

"No, ma'am. I was just leaving to check in with the other officers. See how the details are holding up. Some might need a break, you know?" She nods, and with a quick step, he's out the door. Frankie closes the door behind him, turns around, and leans against it.

"Considering your track record with doors, that might not be a smart idea," I say, turning my body on my desk to face her, my right knee bent and resting on top of it.

"That was one time and after way too many glasses of wine." She takes a few steps into my office and stands arm's length away from me.

"What brings you here, and where is your detail?"

"Getting coffee in the lounge. She's a bit overwhelming. Anyway, I did a preliminary evaluation, and I thought I would bring it here." She hands me a small manila envelope she'd been holding behind her back. "It's not much, but considering all we had to go on, this was the best I could do."

"Thanks, I appreciate it." I take the report and watch as Frankie retreats a few steps to the safety of the door.

"I'll keep working on it tonight, maybe have something more fleshed out by tomorrow." She opens the door with her back gently leaning on it.

"I appreciate it." I stand and Frankie takes a step back.

"Not a problem." She turns to walk out the door.

"I'd feel better if you stayed with me and Chase from now on. You can bring your shadow with you." My voice cracks slightly as I try to hide how vulnerable I feel.

"Considering the situation last night and this morning, I'm not sure that would be appropriate," she says, still facing the hallway.

"Safety in numbers, you know that." I toss out a comment we both know is bogus in this case.

"I'll let you know if I come up with more from the files," she says, but her body doesn't move. I know what her voice is saying, but her body isn't listening.

"Then do it for me," I whisper.

Frankie turns around to face me, her face unreadable, her eyes focusing only on me and her hands clasped in front of her tightly. In response, my breathing speeds up and I feel my body temperature rising with my nervousness.

"Do it for you?" she questions.

"Yes," I say, trying not to give away any emotion.

"Okay, but only if you tell me why."

"If you stayed with me, I wouldn't be worried about you with that guard dog of yours. I'd know you were safe." The words coming out of my mouth are such a mumble of gibberish I doubt Frankie can understand any of it.

"I speak three languages, and whatever you said was not any of them." She crosses her arms in front of her chest.

"If you stay with me, I wouldn't worry about if you were safe or not," I say, clearer than before.

"I have protection courtesy of Officer Mikala Holmes." Frankie smiles again.

"Nothing against the detail of Officer Holmes, but she can't protect you enough for me."

"Jasmine, no one will ever protect me enough for you. It's part of who you are."

"It's because I care about you, okay? Say what you want, Frankie, but I would really appreciate it if you would stay with us tonight. I'll sleep on the couch, but please do this favor for me?"

Her eyes study me for a few moments, and I wonder if she is overanalyzing the situation like I always do.

"I'll come over after my last appointment with Mikala. Maybe we can discuss the profile then."

"Good, I'll let Will know to expect company. It'll be a tight fit, but I'm sure we've got air mattresses somewhere."

Frankie opens the door but stops short of exiting. She looks directly at me. "I never said you had to sleep on the couch."

Before I can answer, she walks out the door, passing Captain Udall as he's coming in. He closes the door behind him, holding a rolled-up paper in his hands. I feel like today is a revolving door of people, and all I really want to do is stare at the damn board.

"Working everything out?" he asks.

"She's helping me break things down." I hold up the envelope and shrug my shoulders.

"I wish you would have told me beforehand." The captain takes a seat across from me. I walk behind my desk and sit down. When I feel a conversation is about to take a darker turn, I prefer having my desk in front of me. It gives me more confidence having a buffer between me and the voice of bad news.

"She's worked with me on several cases before without you being in the loop right away. Any reason why this case is any different?" I ask incredulously.

"Call me naïve, but I was hoping it was for other reasons. It appears the mayor opened his mouth to the higher-ups and the press. The media is breathing down all of our necks regarding these murders. That leads to cranky men in suits and every decision anyone makes being held under a microscope."

"So, they're digging for dirt and the mayor is on the wrong end of it. What has he released to the public?"

"Not much. We've been extremely tight-lipped on this one. That doesn't mean those bastards don't have a way of finding out information. You know that." The captain tosses the paper on my desk. "It's a new day and age. Media can get the word out, get some bit of information truthful or not, and it's everywhere. This case has gone up the ladder to the top, and it made you a higher profile detective."

"Which means what?"

Tyler nods toward the paper. I unravel it and my stomach churns in disgust at the front page.

"Love over justice. Detective Steele pays more attention to her lesbian lover and adopted son than the serial killer terrorizing the city." An older photo of the three of us is plastered in the corner of the page. "You know this is all crap, right?"

"I know that, Jasmine. The pictures, lies, all of it isn't what bothers me. The media is going to be all over you and your family. Everything you do will be scrutinized by the mayor's office and the public. That leaves me with no other option than to put all of you in a safe house, beyond the scope of this office."

"You and I both know Hadley has people on her all the time. You can't stop them all."

"No, but we need to control the crowd. Whoever leaked this information did it with purpose. The more people around you, the less likely we find a specific target. I'm pulling in massive favors. No one will know where you are but your specific details and myself."

"You think it's someone on the inside?" I ask, taking in the new information.

"I've learned a long time ago that when your gut screams at you that something smells funny, don't eat it. I don't have any proof of any misconduct, but I don't like when information leaks from any source. For all I know, the coffee cart chat was overheard and sold. Just tighten the hatches and prevent any further leaks."

"You've been there for me since my family's been gone. You know I'll do what you ask, even if I don't like it," I concede.

"There's more."

"Should I be worried?"

"Garrison is lead on this. He's been in the background on this case, so he can run it with some help."

"He's a prick."

Tyler laughs at me and nods his head in agreement.

"He's a little ambitious, I'll give you that. He's the best man for the job given our situation." Tyler leans forward and drops a business card on my desk.

Picking it up, I see it's the lawyer he recommended when I was dealing with the adoption of Chase. He was a bit more expensive than I could afford, so I went with the cheaper court-appointed one. "What's this for?"

"I know you officially adopted Chase, and I doubt there are any loopholes, but you might want to have him look the paperwork over. Just to make sure."

My stomach is churning, and I can feel the bile rising up from the pits of hell. Tyler looks at me, concerned, but I keep my mouth shut. This cannot be happening.

"There are certain organizations that are making your front page news fuel for their cause to place children into natural loving homes." He waits for me to respond, but I am fighting my stomach and refuse to reply. "They shouldn't have a case, but the reality is those people are going to use you simply because your picture's in the paper. They're not right, but they will cause pain."

I lose control and punch the hard wood drawer of my desk. The sound of cracking bones shocks Tyler, but I feel nothing but calm. I swallow down the acid and look Tyler straight in the eyes.

"If they want a new war, I'll give them one." My voice drips with venom.

"Hold on. We both know they are out of line and frankly so buried in their fear they can't see straight. You can't lower yourself to their level. You have to be stronger, wiser, better than they. You can't give them more fuel."

"I'm breathing, so they have fuel."

"No, you're breathing and living a good life. That makes them angry. Let them have heart attacks figuring out ways to destroy humanity. We have enough stress in our jobs already. Call the lawyer. Have him look everything over, cover your bases, and call it a day. These people can scream to their hearts content—that's their right—but you've got an army of blue behind you. Nothing changes."

"Everything changes, sir."

"You just stay safe, do as I say, and have Will take you to the hospital to get that hand checked out." Udall stands up and remains there as if he wants to say something, but doesn't. Will opens the door and stops short.

"Sorry, sir, I just came by to get Detective Steele." The captain stands and turns his sights on Will. "I expect a decision from you sooner rather than later." He pats the former Marine on the shoulder and leaves.

"Bad day?" Will looks at my hand.

"Nothing I can't handle."

"Right, so red or black?"

I grab my coat and realize how badly I damaged my hand. Will helps me hold my stuff as he leads me out of the office.

"Black. I hear chicks dig the color."

The hospital trip is simple enough. Sitting on the gurney, I realize I'm lucky I didn't do any worse damage. Will teases me the entire time. Hopefully, Frankie won't be too angry with me when I explain my actions. I know I'd be livid with myself. Will's phone rings, and he steps into the hallway. The assistant finishes putting my cast down to my second knuckles and babbles some directions at me. Will comes back into the room.

"Jazz, we need to go, now." His voice is firm, but his eyes show me the truth. Something is wrong, and my stomach is back to being a pit of hell.

Twenty minutes later, we get to the house. Will's arms pull me back into a tight embrace. My house, my home is burning to the ground, and I am unable to do a damn thing about it.

"Chase and Frankie are inside!" I fight against Will, but the man is a Marine. He pulls me closer to his body.

"They were out before the fire started," he whispers so only I can hear him.

It's then the moment clicks for me. I needed to be here to see the fire, to act afraid, so if the killer is watching, he sees me. I stop fighting Will and simply fall to the ground. Everything I own, everything I cherish is gone. Photos, videos, my memories of them—all are gone. There are no tears, just a numbness to it all. The idea of letting go of the past is one thing, but the act of someone ripping it out of your soul is another.

"Detective?" I look up at the fireman in front of me and drag myself to my feet. "The fire has been contained, but it does look like the house is a total loss. The marshal is going to come down and do a more thorough investigation as to the cause."

"I appreciate you talking to me, but I know who did it and why. The how is up to your marshal."

I walk away from the scene in front of me. I can feel the eyes of everyone on me as I fall into the passenger seat of the car. Will slides in a few seconds later.

"How you holding up?"

"I need a drink."

"Everyone's safe."

I nod in response as he pulls the car away from what used to be my home. Everyone might be safe, but my life is now a literal pile of ash.

Chapter Seven

The drive is a virtual blur as buildings pass by, my mind focused on the fact that my entire life history was burned in a matter of minutes. Chase and Frankie were supposed to be safe there. Thankfully, the officers managed to get everyone out in time. It burned so fast an accelerant must have been used. Hopefully, the captain is keeping tabs on the investigators. He'll make sure I'm in the loop.

The elevator doors to the safe house open up, and I feel Will's hand on my lower back guide me into the hallway. The argyle carpet moves by as we quickly walk to a set of double doors. Rather fancy for a lowly NYPD's discretionary budget. I hear Will knock on the door in some Morse code. James opens the door and lets the two of us in.

Hadley sits on a couch in the living area, her knees pulled up to her chest. Victor rests behind Hadley with his arms wrapped tightly around her. Frankie sits opposite them, her hair wet. Chase lies next to her with his head resting on her lap. James closes the door behind us, and it brings everyone's attention our way.

Chase rushes out of Frankie's arms and slams into my legs. His tearstained face looking at me for permission. I kneel down and pull him into me as he breaks down. My cast hits his back harder than I intended. His body shakes as his tears silently hit my shoulder. I pick him up and glance at Frankie. Immediately understanding my unspoken words, she walks to one of the doors in the back and opens it. Wordlessly, I carry Chase past everyone and into the bedroom. The door closes behind me.

With my bad wrist, I move the sheets and force Chase to lay down. He whimpers and pulls at my neck. I pull out of his grasp and bring the sheets back up around him. His tears slow, but his shaking bottom lip does nothing to soothe my soul. Lying down on top of the sheets, he snuggles into me.

"Is everything gone?" he asks with shaky breaths.

"Looks like it."

"I tried to get my photo of Mom and Dad before Aunt Frankie grabbed me, but I couldn't." He whimpers again.

"It's okay, buddy. I have a lot of photos online in the cloud you can have. Might not be the same, but I promise you'll never forget them."

He nods his head and begins to quiet down a bit. He looks over to my black cast and taps his against it. "Wonder Twins . . ." he mumbles, and I'm silently thankful for all the silly cartoons I let him watch on YouTube. "I was scared."

"I know, honey. I was really scared when I saw the house in flames too. I thought you and Aunt Frankie were still inside. Officer Everts had to stop me from running into the house to find you," I say, pulling him tighter to me.

"It started in the kitchen. That's what I heard the officers saying. It moved really fast, like something was helping it run up the walls and things. We had to climb out a back window to get away. It was so hot, like the sun at the beach. Officer Holmes made one call while Hank called 911. Tim was holding Aunt Frankie. She cut herself on the glass when we got out."

"Who was with you?"

"No one. I was good. A black van came before anyone else. We all got in and it brought us here."

"How are you feeling now?"

His eyelids slowly fall. "Sleepy." His body finally gives out. The stress of everything must have been too much on his little body.

"Is he asleep?" Frankie asks from the slightly opened doorway. I nod my head and slither out of the vice grip embrace. I follow her out into the hallway and close the door quietly behind me.

"You broke your hand?" she says, taking my cast in her hands.

"I got into a fight with my desk and lost." I shrug.

"Would it have anything to do with the paper this morning?" she asks, and I look at the others in the living area. Frankie takes the hint and pulls me by my bad hand into an adjoining room.

"No one is taking him; I can promise you that," she says firmly.

"Maybe they won't, but they are going to put up one hell of a fight," I say, allowing some stress from the day to come out. Before I can argue, Frankie pulls me to her. Her head rests on my shoulder, the scent of her freshly shampooed hair fills my nostrils, and her heartbeat radiates through my chest.

"James and Will are going to sleep in the living room. Victor's going to bunk with Chase, Hadley and Mikala have a room, and so do we," she mumbles into me. I don't have the strength to argue. I simply accept the information as it's delivered. "I know you don't want to talk about it, but I will do everything in my power to make sure no one ever takes Chase away from you."

I push Frankie out of our embrace and lead her to the king bed in the center of the room. The two of us sit down, her hands never leaving mine.

"I know you'll fight for me, but you don't have to. I know it's my fight to win. I have to stand up for his well-being."

"I understand what you mean, so I'll let that slide, but you need to accept help when it's given. All of us are a family, and maybe we're not on the same page right now, but you and Chase . . . you mean everything to me. Let me help you, please?" She squeezes my hands tightly in hers.

"I'm sorry my job keeps dragging you into the mud with me. I know I put myself in danger, but this time I've brought everyone into it with me. I really have no idea what I'm doing anymore, Frankie. I have no leads, no evidence . . . nothing. Hell, I don't even have a clean change of clothes."

Frankie lets go of my hands and grabs a small duffel bag from the floor. She drops it on my lap. Unzipping it, I see some of my clothes, important documents in manilla folders, and one of my emergency hard drives.

"I remember you always told me to grab that damn thing on the way out of the house. I listen," she says.

"This is everything I've ever done all backed up. Pictures, movies, work cases . . . We won't forget what they look like," I say, my voice failing me.

"I know. I also managed to convince the driver to make a stop at my apartment. Mikala took me upstairs, and I packed all the things Chase left when he was last there. Plus, I happened to have a few of your things."

"You stole my clothes?" I ask with a smirk on my face.

"Borrowed, Jasmine, don't get it twisted." She smiles again. "Thankfully, the sweats I got him last year that were too big fit him now. He's going to wear a shirt of yours until we can get more clothing."

"Thank you." I touch her cheek. "For everything."

The emotion of the moment takes hold of both of us as Frankie kisses my lips hard. She grasps the back of my neck with one hand, pulling me into her tighter. My hand falls to her hips, allowing Frankie to make all the moves right now.

"Hey, guys . . . oh shit."

Our little moment bursts as Hadley walks into the room uninvited. Frankie blushes, stands, and fixes her clothes as if she could remove the embarrassment by pressing the wrinkles out.

"Is there something you needed, Hadley?" I ask, watching Frankie keep her attention on anything but the two other human beings in the room.

"I was voted off the island and told to come get you two. They want to sit down and have some kind of powwow. Like we haven't talked enough while waiting for Jazz to show up," she says before walking back out of the room. I turn to Frankie, who simply walks out of the room without looking at me.

I follow a few steps behind, making sure to check Chase's room before joining the group. He's managed to twist himself up in all the blankets and he looks peaceful. Thank God for little favors. I turn back into the living room and take a seat next to Frankie on the couch. Will walks in after me and hands me a cold beer. I mutter a thanks, remembering how badly I wanted a drink a little while ago.

"One of my old partners told me the file on the second murder wasn't complete. He said some officer named Garrison found some stuff at the scene, but never logged it," Mikala pipes up from her place next to Victor. "I don't know how he managed to get away with that, but if it's true . . . kid's got something to hide or he's on someone's payroll."

"Or just incompetent." Will adds.

"I scoured the outside of that place. Tried to get in, but a wrestling reject wouldn't let me," I say, taking a sip of my beer.

"Did you check the scene itself?" Will asks.

"No, I was told to walk away by Captain Udall. That's why I looked around the building best I could. Didn't see any forced entry or other obvious signs of a crime," I answer.

"That order had to come from higher up. There's no way he lets that slide," Will continues.

"Did your friend happen to note what Garrison found, Mikala?" I ask.

"He couldn't see what was being picked up, but he did do some digging for me. Turns out that basement was used as a secondary location for B-roll footage for one of Ms. Moreno's films." Mikala looks directly at Hadley.

"Hey, I don't know anything about secondary footage shoots. Unless I'm needed on set at that specific place, I don't know anything. Besides, the producers have location agreements with whoever owns the property . . . if it's a legal one anyway. Maybe the producer handed over the information after you were taken off the case, Jazz. Might not be some big conspiracy, just a misunderstanding," Hadley says, trying to calm everyone in the room.

"Maybe, but the producers provided us with all the locations. Supporting footage or not, this should have been included. Not to mention the producers didn't remove me or want me off their set. I was told in no uncertain terms by the powers that be that under no circumstance was I to enter the basement. You add to that an eye witness seeing Garrison removing items from a crime scene and you have cause for suspicion."

"Or you have paranoia that leads to a big cover-up," Victor adds to the conversation. "Look, I don't think it's precisely about that anyway. It's always about the head of the dragon. Who is pulling the strings in this operation? Contrary to the paper and rumors circulating around, we know Jazz isn't in control. Garrison was given timely information and refused to share it with the class. Steele's house was burned down along with the case files, connections, and theories about this shit. Little more going on in the background, wouldn't you say?"

"Frankie grabbed my wireless hard drive on the way. It's not one hundred percent up-to-date, but it has the majority of the information. If nothing else, we aren't back to square one." I take a sip of my beer and enjoy the cool fluid rolling down my throat. "Had, how are you holding up?"

"Not jumping for joy or anything over here, but what can you do? I have James to watch my back, and that's good, right? I mean he'll keep me safe," she says, trying to put on a brave face. I look over to James, who is more engrossed in his cell phone than what his charge had to say.

"Did you know Garrison was into horror films?" James says, finally looking up. "Apparently, his daddy is like a mega-millionaire and pays for anything his kid wants to do. They invest in all kinds of low-budget horror films that Daddy uses as a tax deduction at the end of the year. Smart."

Hadley's phone beeps softly. She shuts off the alarm, stands up, and grabs her jacket.

"Time to go, fearless protector," she says to James. "I need to go earn a paycheck."

"Overnight shoot . . . Do I get double time for this?" James asks, putting away his phone.

"No, you don't, and Hadley, I think you should stay here. We'd all feel better if you did," I say, leaning forward on the couch.

"Yes, no . . . I don't know." She grabs her jacket and throws it on in a huff. "I have to work, Jazz. They didn't postpone anything for me, and I can't ask them to. The production is already behind schedule because of police activity. They're already not thrilled with me. I don't want to be labeled a difficult actor for the rest of my career."

"Hadley, I understand, I truly do. I still think it's better to have a bad reputation than. . ."

"I get it, okay?" Hadley says her voice firm. "I'm scared shitless, Jazz, but this is my job. These people are after you and Chase. I'm just a pawn in a much bigger game. They aren't calling me or threatening me. You need to stay here to be safe. We have security on location, and James will be there. I'll be fine." Hadley walks out the door before anyone can argue with her again. James rushes out a few steps behind her.

"Now then, what else do we have?" Will asks, trying to bring us all back to the case at hand.

"I think our best lead is Garrison's father," Frankie tosses in before she grabs my beer and drinks some.

"How do you figure that?" Mikala asks.

"He has the means to arrange something like this. Money always leaves a paper trail. People try to cover it up, stash it away, but it eventually shows a direct link. He's the only one that fits the profile of someone with the liquid assets or power to handle something of this scale," Frankie answers quickly.

"I wish you were right, but most of the victims had little or no funds. Our second victim did buy several illegal substances off a dark website similar to Silk Road, but that's it. The productions that Garrison was attached to might be connected to all of this, but we no longer have access to the case to figure it out. At this point, doc, the point's moot." Mikala sits back, defeated.

"Tyler had to put us in a room away from everyone for a reason," I mumble. "So what do we know about Garrison?"

"He's a pain in the ass. Born with a platinum spoon in his mouth. Went to expensive private schools. Never finished college. Couldn't find anything on him being involved with the law," Frankie answers.

"Squeaky clean," Mikala adds.

"Too clean," Will finishes as he reenters the room. "Let's go over this again in the morning; maybe a good night's rest will help."

Victor simply groans in appreciation as he leaves the room. Will props his feet up on the coffee table and holds his beer against his chest. His eyes close.

"Don't spill that," I jokingly say to him.

"Marines never spill."

"See you in the morning, Will." Frankie heads to the bedroom, and I look in on Chase in the room next door. His soft, even breaths fill the room. He looks like he feels safe when he sleeps. I wish I could give him more of that. Closing the door, I walk back into my room.

"Left side of the bed?" I nod as she tosses me a pair of sweats and a shirt. Changing quickly, we both climb into bed. She snuggles into my back as my mind races. "Shut off, Jasmine. We'll figure it out in the morning, okay?"

Just like that I relax and close my eyes.

Chapter Eight

The soft ground below hugs my body as the sun shines brightly above, warming my chilled skin. My puffy red eyes look through sunglasses, staring upwards as if trying to burn away the pain. Salt streaks rest on my cheeks, the collar of my navy-blue button-down school shirt is wet, and my too small heels dig into the dirt as my knees bend. A shadowy silhouette of someone walks into my frame, breaking the light from reaching my eyes.

"Mom send you?" My voice sounds hollow, empty. The shape nods, and I can see the hair flop around. It's my brother, Henry. "Tell her I'm fine, Henry."

He lays down on the ground next to me. His suit is too short for his legs, and his jacket a bit too big. It's hard to find a black suit on such short notice for a kid who still seems to grow taller by the minute.

"You don't look fine," he says softly.

"Looks can be deceiving."

"You're a real pain in the ass, you know that?"

"As your baby sister, it's in the job description," I say curtly. "You can go now."

"You're not a child anymore. Stop acting like one," he responds, his voice full of hurt and anger.

"No, I'm fifteen going on sixty. Nothing like watching someone slowly waste away and die." I turn my attention to my brother, waiting to see what his next response will be.

"It's okay to cry. You haven't done that yet."

"How can you cry when you're too busy consoling everyone else? Getting compliments on how strong you are or how you are such a pillar of strength at a horrible time like this. I think the best one I got was 'ladies don't cry, they process.' Whatever that means."

"Jazz, everyone cries." He pauses, and I turn to see him staring at me.

My brother was raised very differently than I was. He's vibrant; he got more time with my father's side of the family. As the only girl, I was raised to be the glue. We hold everyone together and help them process whatever needs processing. I think the best example was when my mother said, "A good woman stands at the door, ensuring only people who treat your family right come inside." She gets hit with the pain, fear, or ridicule. Whoever remains inside gets to laugh, enjoy life, and never see the darker side. I was raised in that shadowy life.

"Not everyone," I say simply.

"Grandpa was suffering, and now he's in a better place. He's watching us from heaven, just have some faith."

"Faith." I stifle a laugh. "You know, when Monsignor Evans told us about heaven in religion class, I asked if all animals go there. He stumbled over his words and couldn't give me a straight answer. So, I said if every animal, bug, or any of God's creatures that died were there, it would be really crowded. Plus, how could I find Grandpa with a dinosaur or sharks chasing after me? Then he tells me that only people are allowed in. I asked why. I said most people are cruel and have no heart, but my dog was innocent. He had no answer. You know why, Henry? Because there is no heaven. There's birth, life, taxes, inequality, and death. Then, there's nothing. Your brain stops, your memories die, and you are no more. After a few years, you're forgotten just like the generation before you." I gasp a little for air as I finish my diatribe.

Henry stands up and brushes off his perfectly fitting suit. The dimmer, less vibrant sun highlights the wrinkles on the side of my brother's now aged face. A wedding ring is on his left hand, his right at the base of his neck rubbing the stress away.

"You have to stop this!" Henry raises his voice for the first time since I've seen him. "Stop seeing all this darkness and find something positive."

I stand up next to him and wipe the dirt off my pressed police uniform, my rookie tie clipped to my vest, all my accessories making me look like an NYPD Christmas tree.

"How can I do that after all I've seen? All the years of studying mankind, what evil we're really capable of . . . How do you just turn that off? I can't. I still sit in the subway and pick up all the surrounding conversations. I'm always hyperaware. Trust me, it drives Frankie crazy."

"Find a way. See the sun, stars, flowers, or whatever you need. Think of our parents, Mom's laugh at a silly joke or her voice when she sang at my wedding. Think of all the things that make you happy. Focus on the feeling of being in your girlfriend's arms."

"I don't know how to do that."

"You'll learn," he says, patting me on the back before walking up the road to his old house.

The old paver walkway up to the house is as level as the Leaning Tower of Pisa, but Henry put it in himself. Opening the front door, he pushes me inside, where the lights are out but a soft glow emanates from another room. Flipping a light switch on, I see Frankie and Belinda with a birthday cake in the center of the dining room table. Belinda gives me a hug, and Frankie a soft kiss with well wishes.

"You think we'd forget?" Henry says. "Blow out the candles."

It's a tiramisu cake. My favorite. I smirk at my brother before blowing out the candles, engulfing myself in darkness.

The phone rings but I ignore it. I pinch myself, trying to wake myself from whatever dream I seem to be in. The pain radiates up my arm each time I squeeze my skin.

"Descartes said 'I think therefore I am'. So, either this pain means I'm awake, or this is a manifestation of a dream, and I'm creating the pain to stay here. Or I'm in a fucking looney bin, having finally lost my mind."

Closing my eyes, I try to focus on the oxygen going in and out of my lungs slowly. The whole point of anything is to find a way through it. That's what Mom told me after my grandpa's funeral. We have to deal with the situations in front of us and wade through the rest.

The increased brightness forces me to open my eyes. My house is immaculate; the small coffee table clear of any work things. It's homely, but the feeling of pure happiness crawls up my body like osmosis from the floor. A small ring box rests in the center of the coffee table. Looking in the mirror near the door, I see the body-hugging, floor-length black dress complementing my styled hair and makeup. I walk over to the ring box

The phone rings again, making me deviate from my path, and I pick it up.

"Hello?" I ask into the receiver.

No answer.

"Hello?"

A knock on the front door. Hanging up the phone, my heels click as I slowly walk to the front door. I glance at the ring box before opening the door fully and walking outside.

Emergency vehicles scream down the street as the door closes behind me. The sound of my shoes hitting the pavement gets louder as my pace increases, the flashing lights illuminating the entire area in blue, red, and white. A firetruck is off to the side as men in their protective gear rush around in slow motion. The closer I get, the further away it feels. My throat feels dry, swollen, like a severe allergic reaction has taken hold.

Grabbing the yellow tape, I lift it and duck underneath. My right heel slips and snaps, bringing me to the ground. An officer helps me up and his mouth moves, but I hear nothing. My eyes search out anything identifiable by the hive of organized chaos. I pull off my heels and hand them to the officer before walking further into the mess. He grabs my arm, and my hand instantly moves to where my badge would normally be. Feeling the smooth texture of the dress, I simply shake him off and run toward the scene barefoot. The tar feels like it grabs at my skin, painfully holding me from what's there.

"Jasmine, you shouldn't be here." A pair of older hands wrap around my biceps and stop me, holding me in place. Tyler Udall stands there, his face drawn with worried pain etched across it. He looks like he dressed with the lights off as he rushed out of the door. His grip loosens. My eyes look beyond him, and I see the license plate of my brother's car.

"Tell me." My voice wavers, almost begging.

He wraps his arm around my lower back, guides me closer to the scene, and takes a deep breath. I've done that many times before on the job. It's the split second you have to compose yourself before informing people of the worst moment of their lives thus far. That small second allows you to figure out your words and calm your tone. It allows you to control all of the emotions that swirl through you as a human being. You convert from a feeling being to a thing that spits out nothing but black-and-white details. There's no room for gray when you tell someone a loved one has passed.

I feel his hand form a fist behind my lower back, and I can feel it begin to shake a bit. He's struggling, which is the worst-case scenario for me. The factual information and pseudo support will be mired in an emotional mess. His professionalism is slowly cracking, which means I will have to do it for him.

"Just tell me as it is." My voice is firm, cold.

"Your brother and his wife were in an accident," he chokes out.

"Cause?"

"Doesn't matter right now."

"It does to me," I say forcefully.

The smell of gasoline fills my nostrils as the full scene comes into view. Two cars and carnage. A black sports car rests to the side, having been removed from the impact site. The other car is a blue sedan with the driver's side indented severely, the tree causing the most damage on the passenger side.

"Belinda?"

"Passenger . . ." The captain's voice trails off.

My eyes focus clearly and the lights flash off her dark brown hair. My rational brain informs me that she died on impact. The firemen work diligently as they cut the pieces of metal holding up the roof. I see my brother in the front seat ,and for the first time Chase's screams hit my ears.

"Henry?"

"Holding on," the captain says as he nods toward the scene.

I walk through the mess of people barefoot, not caring about any debris around me. The firemen part as I approach, each one of them rushing to the next step on their list to save someone. The doors to the driver's side rest nearby, leaving the side of the car open.

Henry sits in the driver's seat, his head leaning against the headrest. Looking him over, I can see how serious the damage to his body is. The steering wheel is bent down and in, pressing hard against his abdomen below his belly button. Metal from the dash digs into his legs right above the knees, his feet hidden behind a mess of debris, if they're still there at all. Chase exercises his lungs in the back seat as paramedics look him over.

"Hey, ass munch, what you doing here?" I say, kneeling next to my brother.

Henry's eyes flutter open and his head flops forward a bit. He looks to me and blinks a bunch of times. His right eye protrudes forward in the socket as if ready to fall out.

"Hey, shithead, glad you could make it." He smiles, showing his reddened teeth. Blood trickles from the corner of his mouth and meets a stream of blood from a head laceration. "How's Chase?" he asks weakly.

I look over Henry's shoulder to see Chase with a small brace around his neck. A paramedic places an oxygen mask over his face, deadening the sound of his screams slightly. I watch them work him over, checking for any injuries to his extremities. Seeing none visible, I exhale and turn my attention back to Henry.

"He looks okay. Paramedics are taking good care of him. You, however, look like shit," I say, trying to lighten the mood.

"It's just a flesh wound; nothing to worry about." He laughs as he coughs up more blood. His right hand fumbles across the car to Belinda. He grabs her lifeless hand and squeezes it tightly. "Did she say yes? I'm sure she did."

"I'll tell you over drinks when you're better," I say, trying to deflect from the question. It was neither the time nor the place in my mind.

"You didn't ask her."

"Kinda busy coming out here to save your ass." I tap his left shoulder gently.

"They aren't getting me out, Jasmine. You need to take care of my son," he says, fighting to catch his breath.

"Chase has a team of doctors hovering over him right now. Let the guys help you."

"You can't save everyone, not this time." He coughs up more blood, covering his chest in the fluid. I stand up and hit a paramedic in the back trying to get his attention. No one responds to my physical assaults. Henry waves his hand, hitting me a few times, his blood staining my dress.

"Please stay with me," he says, finally grabbing my hand. I kneel back down and pull our clasped hands to my chest.

"I'm not going anywhere." My voice sounds forced, resigned.

"You think Mom and Dad will find me?"

"I'm sure they will."

"If they can avoid all the dinosaurs and sharks, right?" He tries to laugh but ends up coughing.

"Never underestimate our mother. She walked outside in a hurricane to grab us both by the ears and bring us inside. What makes you think she wouldn't find you up there? I'd be afraid for anyone who gets in her way, truthfully." I smile up at him, running my hand through his bloody hair.

"I'm sorry I'm leaving you, sis, but I can't—"

"I know," I cut him off. I look back over the dashboard and understand the reason the paramedics aren't helping him. Everything was being held together by pressure. He's probably been bleeding internally for some time. Once the steering wheel is moved, he'll die. My eyes fix into a lifeless gaze. He has to see nothing but fearlessness and love right now. I can't let him see anything other than that.

Henry's eyes dart to the rearview mirror. He tries to move his hand, but his body is too weak at this point to do much at all. I reach inside the car and angle it so Henry can see his son. I watch a few tears fall out of his left eye as his breathing calms. His blue jeans continue to darken from the wounds. There has to be a good size pool somewhere, and it sends a chill up my spine.

"You ask her. You raise my son with a family. You take care of him. Promise me?" he says through blood bubbles in his mouth, his eyes never leaving the reflection.

"Henry . . ." I say.

He turns to face me, paler, almost lifeless, his face drenched in pain.

"I need to know you're both safe. He needs to be safe." I open my mouth to argue, but he shakes his head. "Promise me!" he grunts as he uses what little strength he has left to pull me toward him.

"I promise." The words fall out of my mouth.

He nods and turns his attention back to the mirror. He smiles as Chase continues to fuss in the back seat.

"Tell him we love him." I can hear my brother's voice crack, and I find my own resolve giving. "Remind him to be a good man. Tell him his daddy trusted you to take care of him because Mommy and Daddy trusted you."

"I will."

Peeking over my brother's head, I see Chase being pulled from the car seat. His arms move around frantically as his cries fill the air. The paramedic hands me Chase. I lean down and hold the younger Steele close to Henry. My brother kisses his son's head, smearing blood on the white skin.

"Daddy loves you, little man. I'll be watching over you, okay?" My brother starts to cry and cough. Blood flows freely from his mouth now.

I hand Chase to the paramedic next to me and grab my brother's hand again.

"I'm scared." His voice is small, broken.

"I'm not going anywhere. I'm right here." I hold his hand so tightly against my chest for comfort.

"I love you, little sister."

"I love you too. You're the best big brother anyone could have asked for."

"You lie"—Henry shakes violently with a coughing fit—"but thanks." Bubbles continue to form in the blood pouring out of his mouth. As quickly as it began, it stops. A banshee-like scream launches from my chest. Leaning into the car, I grab Henry and pull his body close to mine, his blood soaking through my clothing to my skin.

I feel someone pull me back slightly and I fight to stay where I am. Another slight tug, and I find myself on the ground covered in blood. Udall kneels next to me; he's talking, but nothing registers. My eyes stay focused on my dead brother. The captain pulls me to my feet and throws his jacket around me. I watch the paramedics close Henry's eyes as they begin the process of recovering the remains. Randomly, I think both caskets will need to be closed for viewing.

I walk with the captain and notice a police cruiser with the back door open. A younger kid, worn Yankees cap on, head hanging low sits inside, a few officers near the car, watching over him. He must be the other driver.

"Was he drinking?" I say, my voice laced with venom.

"Jasmine, let me handle this. You just take care of Chase. Whatever you need, I'll help you."

"I don't need help. I need my brother alive, and I want some fucking answers!"

"Kid lost control of his car; that's all I know."

"Was he drinking?"

"I don't know anything more than that."

The captain helps me into the back of the ambulance. Chase is lying on a gurney. "I'll call Frankie and have her meet you at the hospital." He closes the doors behind me and taps the back of the ambulance.

Chapter Nine

Bolting upright in bed, I feel the cold chill as the air hits my wet skin. I grab my chest, mentally forcing my heart rate to slow to normal. Looking next to me, I see Frankie still sound asleep, her hair to the side, one leg exposed and on top of the sheets. Her breathing is even and her face peaceful. I wish I could sleep like she does. In the beginning of our relationship, that bugged me, but now I'm thankful for it.

My cell phone vibrates against the wood end table noisily, radiating through the suite. I grab the offending object and slide across the screen to answer as I walk into the bathroom for privacy.

"Hello?" I whisper.

"Good morning, detective. It's been awhile." The voice on the other end cuts me to the bone. All the uneasy feelings from my nightmare increase when the reality of my situation comes to light.

"What do you want?" I say, trying to hide the nerves in my voice.

"Maybe I just want to have a conversation. Why does it always have to be about desire? Unless there's something you're not telling me, detective," the voice taunts me.

"I just want to know what you want. I'm tired of playing these games," I say, my voice a little firmer than before.

"I'm rather enjoying this game. How are you coming along with trying to find me? I'm sure the lack of evidence has left you reeling."

"If you're so hell-bent on me finding you, just tell me where you are."

"Detective, whoever said I was that far away from you? You want answers, but you have yet to look at what's right in front of your face. Why should I give you everything? What would you have done if the captain couldn't hold your hand through everything that you've been through? I truly wonder if you would have succeeded as much as you did," the voice says through the phone, a slight anger leaching into every word.

"What does it matter where I am and how I got here?"

I hear him laugh in the background somewhat satanically. I feel myself squeezing the phone as if I was squeezing the life out of the caller. If my hands could be around his throat right now, I doubt I would stop until he was dead. No evidence, no paper trail, just torment. It's as if this case is a beginning, the first book in Lord of the Rings. No matter how interesting the story as a whole might be, the first book is boring shit.

"Tell me, Jasmine, have you ever just wanted to fade away into nothing? Maybe just pack up your life and go away without telling your family where you are?"

"Everybody has. What's your point?" I say, irritation taking over.

"Well see, that's the problem. No matter what I do, no matter what I say . . . you just don't seem to want to go away. I've worked just as hard as you. Put in as many hours as you and what do I have to show for it? How many years are you going to make me suffer for a mistake?"

Looking at my tired reflection in the mirror, his words hit my heart and shatter into pieces. I don't think he meant to slip like that. It could be any number of mistakes or reasons why I am involved, but my gut tells me something very different.

"I remember everything about that night. I remember your worn baseball cap, the Yankees logo gray with dirt and wear. You were so drunk that you couldn't stand up, let alone hold your head up in the back of the cruiser. After my brother died, Tyler walked me to the ambulance where my nephew was. He held me back from attacking you. He stopped me from punching you in the face so many times that every bone would be broken. The captain protected you just like he protected me from making a dumb mistake. For the rest of your life, you'll have two bodies on your soul. You might've worked as hard as I have, but you got slaps on the wrist in a sealed record. I got a cemetery plot and a child. I get to see your face every day at work reminding me that murderers do walk free. You're the fuel for my career. One day Karma is going to come for you, Garrison, and I'll be eating popcorn." I say, my voice low and dripping with vengeance.

"Congratulations, you actually are a detective. This whole thing isn't just about me, Jasmine. It's about what's right. You couldn't just leave well enough alone." His voice is normal, even. After all of my threats, he's still stone cold. How he managed to pass the police psychiatric exam, I'll never know.

"Where are you?"

"Does it really matter? I have ears to the ground, money to throw at people to do my bidding, and a father who doesn't need a dark spot on his family record. You should be thanking me, detective. You said it yourself, I'm your fuel. You could still be pushing tickets or be a meter maid. Hell, I could've been your boss." A slight chuckle comes through the line.

"Tell me where you are, and I'll show you how truly thankful I am." The threat pours out of my mouth before I can stop it.

"I just told you, I have people working for me. You make it sound like I'm alone in this endeavor. Trust me, I have help. I'm exactly where I'm supposed to be. I get to watch a beautiful scene unfold full of blood, gore, and the little death. Some cheerleaders about to be slaughtered, I think. God, I love these films. They give me such a rush in all the right places." His voice lowers to the point I can hear Hadley's fake scream in the background.

The realization hits me like a ton of bricks. He's on the movie set right now. James should be nearby to delay him, but Garrison's not a fool. He's set everything up perfectly; he'll be ready for this.

"If you hurt her . . ."

"You'll do what?" I can hear his cockiness radiating through the phone. "You'd actually have to be here, and I think I have a bit of a head start. But who knows, maybe you'll get lucky." I hear Hadley's voice in the background getting louder, closer. "Then again, maybe not."

The phone line goes dead. I immediately go into mindless action. I walk into the bedroom as silent as I can be and collect my clothes from the night before. I grab my holster and ensure my weapon is in it, fully loaded. Digging through my duffel bag that Frankie brought me, I find my ankle pistol and attach it to my leg. I hear her moan of annoyance come from the bed, and I stop all my movement. Waiting a few seconds to ensure that Frankie's still asleep, I get fully dressed.

Looking back over my shoulder, I wonder if she'll forgive me for walking out the door again. In the living room, Will's passed out on the couch. Knowing his past in Afghanistan, I walked gingerly to not alert him to a change in his surroundings. Lifting the keys to his car from the tray by the door, I slip out of the safe house and into the unknown.

I slam the button of the elevator frantically, begging it to move faster. Thoughts of Hadley fill my mind, terrifying me of what he could be doing to my friend right now. It's moments like these that time seems to fly yet remain so slow. When the doors finally open, I walk inside and once again beat the garage level button into submission.

Unlocking my phone, I quickly dial James. I'm hoping for an answer, but receive none, his voicemail almost mockingly asking me to leave a message. I hang up and dial again. The same chipper voice graces my eardrums like nails on a chalkboard. When the doors open again, I rush to Will's car and hop inside. I try dialing James again but get the same result. I toss my cell phone into the passenger seat, frustration building in my gut.

Even in the city that never sleeps, traffic seems to come to a lull in the wee hours of the morning. Running several red lights, zigzagging through what few cars are on the road, I make it to the deserted film set in about fifteen minutes. I barely get the car in park before rushing out of it and onto the set. My first red flag: no one's guarding the entrance. The hairs on the back of my neck stand up, and I know I should call backup, but who can I trust?

The floodlights from the shoot illuminate the tall buildings but create shadows between the trailers. The ominous look reminds me of that Stephen King novel with the clown that my brother and I were terrified of. Those shadows provided anywhere to hide, ambush, or attack. Taking a deep breath, I pull my gun out and take the safety off. Slowly, I walk into the darkness and wait for my eyes to adjust. The voices of actors echo around me. Random dialogue, laughter, and a director yelling "cut" reach my ears. None of them are Hadley.

Slithering around the trailers, my eyes search for the gold star. Every corner I turn, I have my gun at the ready. On occasion, I duck down to the floor to ensure nobody's hiding underneath. Finally seeing Hadley's trailer, I look at my surroundings before rushing to the door. Grabbing the handle, I turn the knob slowly. I barely get the door open before James pops out, startling me and nearly getting shot.

"What the hell are you doing in here? Why aren't you with Hadley?" I whisper frantically to him.

"Jesus." He takes a step back with his hand on his chest. "She's on set. I wasn't allowed to go with her. If you give me a second to catch my breath, I'll take you there."

I turn away from the door and put my gun back in its shoulder holster. James takes a few steps down out of the trailer, his gun on his belt with his cuffs.

"Did you put your safety on?" he asks me. I simply shake my head in reply. "You know Hadley hates making a scene with this crap. You don't want somebody grabbing your gun instead of a prop by mistake and killing someone. Put the damn safety on."

"I think I'll leave it off, thanks. I know he's here, and I don't want anything standing in my way of taking a shot if needed. Nobody will be able to get my gun away from me, I promise."

"Whatever, just don't piss off the bigwigs," he says, walking two steps in front of me. I notice his cell phone clipped on the other side of his belt.

"Why didn't you answer your cell phone?"

"Director told me no cell phones on set. Something about interference with the microphones," he says nonchalantly.

"You didn't think to check in? Maybe send a text message and let us know why your phone would be off?" I answer harshly.

"No. I thought I had it handled. Did something happen?"

James and I walk around the major set builds and head to a large brick building in the back, the voices from the cast and crew long gone from my earshot. The hairs on the back of my neck slowly creep to a stand and my stomach rumbles as acid pours into it. Something's not right, but I'm not quite sure what that is.

"I got another call. Where are we going? The sets are back there," I say, my voice lower, almost accusatory.

"To see Hadley. She's in the green room," he says, walking a little faster ahead of me. His voice wavers ever so slightly, and for the first time, I'm questioning his loyalty. The way he walks ahead of me, ignoring my questions and constantly looking around, is creating suspicion within me. It's something I never noticed before, and I should have. It's like a snake oil salesman or financial planner making their millions off churning your retirement accounts. There is a smarmy aura around them, but if you're not in tune to it, you don't see it. My antenna is raised and I'm focused on the right channel, but I'm already following him to God knows where. I really wish I called for backup.

Walking up to what looks like a garage door, James peers through a small window and waves. After a few seconds of standing there, he knocks in something sounding similar to Morse code. Listening to the reverberation of the sound lets me know the warehouse is hollower on the inside than it appears.

"I thought they were filming," I say, trying to hide the concern in my voice.

"Nah, that's why I looked in the window first. They're just being annoying and not answering the damn door," he says, a little anger seeping into his tone.

"If you say so."

James takes a step away from the door and shakes his head. Moving past him, I glance through the window and see nothing but debris. Stacks of crates, wooden pallets, and other garbage litter the floor, making it a maze of sorts. The biggest thing missing is the crew and all film equipment. It's then that I realize Garrison wasn't just talking about the crew of the film being on his payroll. James is in his pocket as well.

"What are you doing, James?" I say, not turning around. I hear the click of his gun and feel the nozzle press into the back of my head.

"What I was hired to do," he says, pushing the firearm harder into the base of my skull.

Before I can say anything further, the garage door comes to life. Slowly, methodically, it cranks and squeals. With every second that passes my blood pressure rises. I know who's behind that door, but what they're going to do is anyone's guess. After an agonizing few seconds, the door stops, revealing no one behind it. The shock must be evident on my face, but James doesn't see it. I still have both my weapons on my body currently. If he's smart, he'll takes my sidearm before we go in there. No one knows about my ankle piece; it was always more for moral support than use.

He pushes me forward, forcing my chin to hit my chest. My legs move a few steps before I feel him push the gun into my head again.

"Stop." I feel the nozzle of his weapon move off my scalp, followed by the telltale sound of the door closing behind us.

"You sure you want to do this? There's no coming back from it," I say, hoping for the best but expecting the worst.

"We all have our roles to play, detective. Personally, I'll be relaxing in a country with no extradition when this is over. No assholes spitting on me when I ask a simple question. Nobody recording my every move because I wear a uniform with a badge. Total and utter freedom from the disrespect that comes with being a member of the NYPD. Plus, enough money to buy whatever whore I want," he says, pushing his weapon back against my head to emphasize his point.

"Garrison's father paid you," I say matter-of-factly.

"Of course, he did. You think the son has any power in this game? You're a fool if you think he does. It doesn't matter anyway. I'm gone in less than twenty-four hours."

"That is if you live to see tomorrow morning," I say with venom in my voice. It's unlikely I'm getting out of here alive, but why not scare the little shit while I'm here.

"Keep telling yourself that. In the meantime, take your gun out of the holster and kick it behind you," James demands. "Don't try anything stupid or your brains will be on the garbage before your body hits the floor."

I grab my gun slowly with my right hand before leaning to the right side and placing it on the ground. I kick it ever so slightly behind me. If he bends down to pick it up, I can overpower him in three moves or less.

"Kick it back further or I put a bullet in your head," he responds to my tactics.

I comply, pushing the gun further away from me. I can hear the metal scrape on the ground, and his gun leaves my head for a second when he picks up mine. I assume he put my gun in his holster for safekeeping. I feel his breath on my neck, his weapon in my back as his hands roam up and down my body, frisking me. He takes his time, enjoying every sweep past my breasts and in between my legs. It's demoralizing, demeaning, and it's meant to be. When he reaches down my right leg, he stops at the ankle. I feel him lift my pant leg up and remove my small sidearm.

"You should've told me you had more than one. Here I am being honest with you and you're lying by omission. What else are you hiding? Where else are you hiding it?" His hand with my weapon slides back up in between my legs and he grabs my crotch hard. "Maybe I should strip search you. See how you like it."

"You're a cop. You know we never travel with just one," I say, trying to keep my cool.

"Always a smart-ass," he says.

Before I can say anything else, I weight of the weapon smacking me in the side of the head. I put my hands out in front of me to lessen the pain of my fall. My cast hits first, cracking. My hand pulses with pain as I lie there on my side. I look up at James as he stands over me ominously. He grabs my right arm, flips me to my stomach, and presses his knee in my back. Holding me in place, I hear the metal of his handcuffs before he latches them onto my wrists. The pain radiating up my arm makes me want to scream, but I don't give him the satisfaction. He grabs the metal and pulls me up by the handcuffs. I look over my shoulder and lock eyes with him for the first time. The slightly red hue flowing into my eye indicates blood from a cut on my forehead. His eyes are lifeless, cold. There is no redeeming him now.

"Maybe next time you won't be such a bitch." James pushes me forward toward the back of the building. After we stumble down a flight of stairs, he opens a heavy steel door and throws me inside the pitch-black room. I hear the door creak and slam behind me. I kick the door frantically until the sounds of soft crying permeates my brain.

"Who's there?" I ask the darkness.

"Jasmine? Is that you?" Hadley's voice responds.

"Hadley? Where are you?" I feel around with my feet, trying to gauge my surroundings. The room is much larger than I expected and getting my bearings seems moot. Laying on my back and slithering like a snake until I hit a wall seems to be the best way to maneuver in here. I keep going like that until I hit a lump in the corner. I feel the mass move as if shocked by my touch.

"Had, if that's you, I want you to grab my leg," I say. I'm not sure if what I hit is truly alive or someone who died recently. Sounds far-fetched, but this whole scenario is fucking crazy. I feel a shaky hand on my leg, and I know she's next to me. "I want you to slide your hand up my body to my arm and help me sit upright."

Hadley does as I ask, and I try to slither against the wall but I find another form. Fumbling with my handcuffed hands, I feel around for any signs of life. I find none.

"Who was in here with you?" I ask, not really wanting the answer.

"My assistant, Miranda," she sputters between frantic sobs. I feel her arms wrap around me and her head lands in the nook of my shoulder, her tears soaking my skin and shirt. "She was just helping me. Then James came in and just . . ." Her voice fails and she cries some more.

"Just take a breath, okay? I need you to calm down and tell me what happened," I say soothingly.

She leans back, and I can hear her breathing coming back to normal. She keeps her hands folded together on my lap. I guess the touch of another human being in a stressful situation is comforting.

"I was working on a really annoying scene in my trailer. I had James running lines as the villain. One minute everything was fine, and the next minute he starts changing the dialogue. He started talking about a beach in another country and the promise of never having to do trashy films again. He kept saying I was better than that and my body was a temple to him. I thought he was being funny, and I laughed it off. Told him it wasn't in the script, but he could write one if he wanted. Next thing I know he grabbed me by the arms hard. He told me he wanted us to leave right now. Something about protecting me from the real enemy and giving me everything I've ever wanted. Then he kissed me, and I fought like hell against him," she said, her voice a mix of anger and fear.

"Did he tell you who the real enemy was?"

"No. I didn't take him seriously. He was my detail, you know? Shit like that only happens in the movies, not in real life."

"What happened next?" I asked, pushing a little harder.

"I politely refused, but he wouldn't let go of me. I figured denying his kiss and advances was enough, but apparently, I was wrong. I made him sing in an octave or two higher than he normally does when I kneed him in the balls. Once he let go, I ran out of my trailer. I must've gotten twenty feet from the main set before someone with a gun stopped me."

"What did he look like?"

"Slightly shorter than James, built differently . . . Darker hair, green eyes, not as muscular."

"That's good. I'm amazed you got all that," I say, surprised.

"I'm an actress, not an idiot. Besides, that was the last thing I saw before someone hit me over the head. I figure it must've been James since I've only heard two voices out there. This room is a really big echo chamber."

"And Miranda?"

"I woke up with her in here. She said she saw me being dragged away and tried to stop them. The shorter one was angry that we were talking. He opened up the door, and In what little light we had, I watched him snap her neck. She didn't deserve that," Hadley says with emotion creeping back into her voice.

Before I can continue the line of questioning, the door swings open and the lights turn on, blinding us both. Squeezing my eyes shut tightly, I try to adjust them quickly. Not being able to see has made me defenseless to the hands fumbling at my handcuffs. I hear them unlatch and rub my broken wrist. Within seconds my arms are pulled forward and handcuffed in front of my body.

My eyes finally adjusting, I make out the shape of a tall man in front of me—James. He grabs a metal hook and hangs the chain of my cuffs on it. Hitting a button, the hook rises, taking my arms with it. He holds a gun on Hadley, effectively preventing me from fighting back. After what seems like an eternity, my tippy toes leave the ground. My wrist screams in agony as my mind tries to block it out.

"Couldn't think of a more unique torture?" I cough out to James. He responds by punching me in the stomach. I hear Hadley in the background begging him to stop. I look up and smile at James before spitting in his face. His fist hits my right eye, and I feel something give way. A metallic taste fills my mouth, and I spit it out at James. His shirt now covered with blood-filled saliva, his face remains stoic and unresponsive. He pulls back his right arm and begins pounding my chest and stomach, forcing me to cough up more blood. Hadley continues to scream, but it makes no difference.

"Enough," a voice says.

Just like that, James stops. I feel my body swing a bit like the carcass of a cow after slaughter. I'm not sure what's going to happen next. One thing's for sure: my body can't take much more of this. I have to get a plan together to get the two of us out of here.

"Long time, detective."

Letting my eyes focus on the figure behind James, I see the worn Yankee's cap from my nightmares. Garrison stares at me, his eyes tired and face unshaven.

"You look like shit," I manage to say with what little energy I have left.

"You've made it a little more difficult than it had to be. What did you expect?" He hands a rag to James. "You're wanted in the other room."

James wipes the blood off his hands as he walks out of the room. Garrison stands there stoically as if waiting for me to start the conversation. I can't be bothered; I'm more focused on staying awake.

"You couldn't just let me handle it? You had to be the big bad detective."

"My phone kept going off and threatening my family. What did you expect me to do?" I mumble.

"Sorry about that. James has proven to be a bit overzealous at times."

"You're telling me James was the voice on the phone? I don't buy it."

"I'm saying he could've gone a little easier on your beating," he says, turning my face to the side to survey the damage.

He lets go of my face before kneeling next to Hadley. I struggle against my restraints, but my legs just swing in the air. He brushes his hand along the side of her face, pushing a stray hair behind her ear.

"You weren't supposed to be involved, and for that I'm sorry. It'll all be over soon." He smiles before smacking her in the head, knocking her unconscious. Standing, he turns his attention back to me. "All you had to do was let things go. This is all on you."

"If this is all on me, I'll accept that," I say, trying to catch my breath. "Only if you come clean about killing my brother and his wife."

"Ruin my career on a mistake I made as a stupid kid? I know what I did was wrong. I see their faces every time I close my eyes, and that's my cross to bear. But you . . . you want revenge. That's premeditated."

"You need to be held accountable for what you've done. I don't care how much money your father has or who he's paid off. You're still a murderer."

"My father . . ." Garrison begins to pace, running his fingers through his hair. "He's not a man you cross or disappoint. If you owe a debt, it's never paid no matter what you do."

"You're telling me that you're doing this because you're in debt to your daddy?" I laugh as the blood drips out of my mouth to the floor.

Without missing a beat, Garrison punches me in the face. He shakes his hand in the air as I continue to laugh at him. Between his weak handshake and his even weaker punches, I know all I need to know about Keith Garrison. He's a pathetic little man with no honor, loyalty, or compassion for anyone other than himself.

"Your friend brought this upon herself. If she had just said yes to his invitation, none of this would've happened. She would've gone on one date, maybe slept with him, and then moved on. Then James wouldn't have had to follow you, call you, or harass you to figure out what you knew. It all just got so out of hand. She spreads her legs for a stupid movie, but not for a man who could kill her? Why can't actresses just be the whores they were meant to be?" he says, anger radiating off him.

"Maybe because your father wasn't her type and she has more respect for her body than that. Not everyone is a plaything."

"You don't get it, do you? If she had said yes, my father wouldn't have been home that night. Instead, he got drunk and ridiculed me for being a piece of shit son and a waste of space. I wouldn't have gone to the bar and gotten plastered. Then, I wouldn't have driven home and killed your family. So, you see, she shouldn't have been involved, but it is all her fault. Then, you just had to keep putting your nose where it didn't belong. Don't you get it now? There's so many loose ends, and my father doesn't like that. This isn't going to end well for any of us."

"If it makes you feel any better, she said no to James too. Then again, she says no to all her crazy stalkers. That doesn't matter though, right? I mean nothing is your fault in this situation according to you. Nothing's Daddy's fault either. Everything falls on Hadley or me. Why not just kill us right now?"

His eyes burn a hole into me, but he says nothing. With his left arm, he reaches out and grabs the motorized contraption that lifts or lowers the hook. He presses a button, and my feet finally feel the floor again. I stumble to gain my balance, and I feel a bit lightheaded. He stops the machine when I'm low enough for him to remove the handcuffs. Unlocking them, he grabs my broken wrist hard, effectively keeping me in place.

"I'm good at a great many things, detective." He picks up my cast, breaking it off the best he can. "The most exhilarating sport I love is hunting. It's just you and your prey." He pushes me against the back wall, and I bring my wrist to my chest. "I hope you understand I have a job to do. There's a limited amount of space here. Not much in the way of hiding or escaping. I'm sure you'll give me a run for my money."

"Ready?" James says as he pops his head back in, disrupting the two of us.

Garrison gives James a cold, hard stare, one that makes me shiver, before nodding in response. I watch as James's eyes fall to Hadley's prone form on the floor. I see a hint of compassion and anger as he looks back at Garrison.

"I'm not going to make this easy for you. I'll make sure they put you in your dress blues when we are done," I say, smiling confidently.

James places a small egg timer near the corner of the door. It ticks away melodically, and Garrison rolls his eyes almost in pleasure.

"It's set for one minute. After the time expires, it will disarm the traps I have in this room. Then, you can leave. Once you do, the hunt is on and we kill you both." James walks in and lifts the unconscious Hadley off the floor and carries her out of the room. Garrison reaches down and winds up the timer to ensure I have a full minute before leaving.

I look around the room, frantically searching for where these traps could be placed. Part of me wonders if he's full of it, testing me to see if I'll break his rules. Keith Garrison has never been one for order or structure; whether he would start now is the question. Regardless of what my head says, urging me to try, I can't risk Hadley's life. Listening to the ticktock of the seconds passing by, I realize that once again time is moving so fast yet also sputtering slowly with my anxiety.

Chapter Ten

After what seems like an eternity, the minute passes and the timer rings loudly. The fact that they took Hadley with them concerns me. I've had a full minute to sit and ponder my next move. Grabbing the discarded handcuffs, I use the edge to help rip the rest of my cast off. At this point in time, I need all the help I can get, and having my hand restricted is useless. The building is bigger than it appeared on the outside, and my first priority is to stay alive long enough to get Hadley out of here.

Looking around the barren room, I see nothing that could be used as a weapon. The minute I walk out that door, I could get hit with a gunshot to the head. I need to protect myself. For now, I guess I'm stuck with my good looks and wit. In other words, I'm pretty much screwed.

Hesitantly, I peer out the door and gauge if it's safe. The main room still looks the same. Crates and boxes litter the floor; some stack all the way to the low-lying catwalk. There's a staircase at the other end that I can barely make out in the shadows, and one to my left. Based on the layout I can see, I'm either a sitting duck on the floor or a hawk in the sky. Normally, I would choose the vantage point of being high up. Without my gun though, that might defeat the purpose. Being on the floor I can zigzag through the stacks and maybe even create places to hide. Up above, you have a clean shot at me.

My decision made, I start to walk into the main area, staying as low as possible. My breathing is steady, steps slow, my focus sharp. If he's going to hunt me, I'm going to make damn sure it's difficult.

"Get the fuck off me!" Hadley's scream echoes off the walls of the warehouse. It immediately changes my decision, and against my gut, I make for the staircase to the upper level.

When I get to the top, I slowly ease around the corner to see what might be there. Surprisingly, it's empty. Following the wall, pressed up against it, I see two doors at the end of the hallway. Hopefully, they're empty of assailants but will provide some kind of weapon. Any piece of garbage at this point would do. There's no way I can head to the other side of the catwalk without one.

Coming to the first door, I fumble for the doorknob and turn it slowly. Opening the door without making a sound, I slip inside and close it behind me. The room is a wasteland for old desk parts. Broken chairs, a splintered piece of the table, and various metal legs litter the floor. Grabbing the metal bars, I try to snap them off the chair, to no avail. Grabbing one of the executive desk chairs, I flip it over quickly and pull the five-star wheelbase off. I grab the bar connecting the seat to the wheels and hold it in my right hand. It's a shady distance weapon, but up close it'll pack a punch.

Walking back into the hallway, I head to the next door across the hall from me. Once again, I open it as slowly as possible to avoid making a noise and slip inside. The room is dark, and I fumble on the wall for a light switch. Feeling something similar to the shape and style, I flip it. A light flickers above, illuminating what appears to be blood spatter all over the back wall. Touching it proves my suspicion is accurate; whatever happened is recent as the fluid is still wet.

My mind reels at the thought of who this blood could belong to. Looking over the splatter design, I determine the person was taller, or the angle was upward. Looking at the floor, I see some brain matter or some other flesh in the blood. They were executed, and the body moved. Not abnormal, but not rational when in a place like this. Nobody would know or care if a body was in an abandoned warehouse. It would look like a drug deal gone wrong or maybe a sexual encounter that ended on the wrong side of the pistol. The point is, there's no reason to move the body. I still come back to my first question though: Whose blood is it? Seeing nothing else of note in the room, I flip the light switch off and head back to the hallway.

I hear Hadley's voice once again, and my feet move faster than before. The main room below seems so much darker and more ominous.

So many places to hide down there, and my mind is playing tricks on me. Looking across the catwalk, I realize I have to stay as low as humanly possible to get across safely. Kneeling down, I start to make my way to the other side. The lights above create some shadows that pull my attention every now and again. Some movement catches my eye at the other end. I slow my progression and wait. Whatever it is, it isn't moving now.

Once I make the intersection above the main floor, I take another look around below me. It would be so much easier if I had my night vision goggles and my gun. I'd just run down the walkway with no care in the world. I'm not sure if the other walkways lead anywhere, and I'd rather not find out. I continue to the other side, slow and steady, making as little noise as possible.

The slight creaks of the bolts and screws holding these metal contraptions up emanates from every step I make. These old buildings originally didn't have cables for support. It was a safety feature added much later on. In other words, if those bolts give way, I hit the floor hard. Exhaling a breath I didn't know I was holding, I continue across. It's quiet. Too quiet for my taste and my fear. Garrison said he loved to hunt. He was good at it. He's probably lying in wait until the perfect moment to strike. I have to figure out when that is.

Finally getting off the rusted metal deathtrap, I slide across the hallway and press my back against the wall. Noise in the room behind me brings my attention to the forefront. Grabbing the bar as tightly as I can, I open the door, staying low. If they're going to fire a shot, it'll be chest level. Hopefully, it will give me enough time to fight back. I slip inside, waiting for an attack that never comes. Some flickering lights on the back wall highlight a small section of the room. Staying crouched, I make my way over there to investigate why they're on.

It's then that I see her heels, one broken and one missing. Hadley's form-fitting jeans are torn and dirty, her belt missing and her shirt askew. Her bleach-blonde hair is matted and covered in filth. There's a little bit of dried blood in there too, and it breaks my heart. The worst part of it all is she's not moving. Dropping to my knees, I gently roll Hadley over and check for a pulse. Finding a stable one, my heart rate slows to normal.

"Hadley?" I whisper as I gently shake her to wake her up. "Hadley, I need you to wake up," I continue. My hands run through her hair, checking for a worse head trauma than before. All the blood is dry, caked to her skin and hair. "Hadley, please wake up."

I use all of my strength to force Hadley into a sitting position. Leaning her up against the wall, I keep her head upright and tap her cheeks a little with my free hand. She slowly mumbles, as if not wanting to wake up to go to school. I continue tapping her face while whispering in her ear to get up. I don't have time to be nice, but I don't want to hurt her any more than she already is.

"Jasmine?" she groggily replies as her eyes flutter open. I grab her arms to stop them from flailing about and hold her in place. When her eyes finally focus on me, I let go.

"How badly are you hurt?"

"I have a headache. Like a really bad headache. Feels like one of our bad hangovers from college times infinity." She coughs a bit, and I wait to see if blood comes out of her mouth. Moving her lips with my hand, I see none. She swats away my hands. "Stop shoving your hands in my mouth. I don't know where they've been."

"I heard you screaming. What happened? Are you sure you're okay?" I ask again, worry radiating off me.

"You look like shit," she says, deflecting. Her hand touches just below my eye and a burning pain sears into my brain. All this time the adrenaline's been preventing me from feeling the full extent of the pain. It doesn't help when your friend pushes on it though.

"I didn't scream, I swear. The last thing I remember was being in a room with you watching you get your ass kicked." It's then that I hear movement below, making the pain fade to the background. I should have realized Hadley was the cheese, and I was the mouse. I walked into a trap.

"We need to get out of here now!" I say, pulling Hadley to her feet. She struggles a bit, and I slide my good arm around her and try to drag her away. "I need you to move Had; they're coming."

I feel her carry more of her own weight as we shuffle to the door. Pulling it open, I see James standing in the hallway. I remove my arm from around Hadley and try to stand up tall. His eyes rake over my body while I hear Hadley sharply inhale.

"Miss me?" James says with a sinister sneer on his face.

Wasting no time, I charge at him and tackle him to the ground like my brother taught me—shoulder to the chest, straight to the ground.

"Hadley, run!" I scream back at my friend, hoping she listens.

I press the small metal pipe across James's throat, effectively cutting off his oxygen. Hadley carefully gets around us and runs down the stairs. James takes my diverted attention as a sign it's time to fight back. He punches my swollen face, knees me in the chest, and rolls me over. His hands grip the bar and press it down hard. I struggle to push up with my right hand to relieve the pressure on my throat.

"It was fun taunting you, detective, but you still should have stayed out of it. I always knew you were a pompous prick, always out to save everyone." James leans back slightly, allowing me to gasp for air. "I wonder how I'll explain this to your friends. Especially Frankie, that'll be fun. Maybe she'll lean on me to help her through such a terrible time. I'll end up consoling her so much she decides to drive stick again. I want the last thing you think of in this world to be me fucking your girlfriend."

Anger is a ridiculously powerful tool at your disposal every day of your life. There's a rage that women have that no man could ever counter. You come after our children or our family and we make the Incredible Hulk look like a pansy. Swinging my legs upward, I latch them around his chest and fling him to the ground. Before he can move, I lock my ankles and begin to squeeze. He continuously punches my knees, thighs, and anywhere else he can reach. I grab the small bar that's fallen to the ground next to us and hit him in the face.

His moan ekes out of his mouth like a child learning to speak for the first time. The thought of Frankie being taken by this man enrages me, and I hit him again and again. Blood gurgles in his throat, and I loosen my grip with my legs. Bubbles form as he tries to say something, but the point is moot. His right arm weakly swings at me, barely touching my skin. I hit him again with such force I hear his skull crack. No more moaning. No more punches. I turn to the side and violently throw up pure acid, knowing full well what I've done.

His face is barely recognizable. His eyes vacant and tinged red, blood pooling by my leg below him. With everything that I have, I push his body off me and slide away. My pants are stained, some brain matter on them. I killed a man. I've never raised my gun and fired. I've never needed to hit someone for survival. Staring at James's lifeless body, I watch the blood expand on the crappy floor. It's an odd sight, watching all the fluids leave a bod. Slowly, like water in the great flood, it overwhelms the garbage nearby, swallowing it within the pool.

I hear a door close below me, and it forces my attention back to the game at hand. This is what Garrison wanted. He just proved that anyone is capable of murder regardless of why it was done. The idea that I might have to do it again forces what little bile is left in my stomach to make an appearance. I wipe my mouth on my dirty sleeve and lean forward to pat down the body. I feel a small pocketknife in the front of his pants and pull it out. Part of me wishes he had his gun, but if he had, I would've been dead before I got anywhere near him.

Standing up, my shoes slip in the blood on the floor. Using the wall for support, I walk to the main catwalk. I'm not thinking about the height or the possibility of being shot. The adrenaline coursing through my veins has made me feel a bit invincible. I also don't know if Hadley has made it out alive. I have to create a diversion to ensure she has extra time. If that means I'm going to die, that sucks, but we do what we have to do.

I jog across the catwalk, making as much noise as possible. The metal clangs and shudders with every step. I wonder if he's watching me from the floor below. When I get to the end, I turn around and run back. This time my footfalls are harder and louder. I'm trying to be like that carnival game where when you hit the bear, it turns around and goes the other way. It gets boring after a while. If you're a true hunter, it's not fun if somebody is sacrificing themselves. There is no thrill in the chase or control over your prey.

Reaching the back staircase after my fourth trip across the catwalk, I loudly walk down the stairs. I start humming a random tune that my mother used to sing to me when she would tuck me in. I don't remember the words, they were in German, but the tune is simple. I get to the bottom of the stairs and stop. Leaning on the railing, I open the pocketknife. The blade is shiny and reflective, but most of all sharp.

"At the end of the day, we're all just dust in the wind." I can hear my father singing the wrong words to various tunes in my head. "You hear me, Garrison? It's all pointless anyway!" I scream at the top of my lungs.

Looking ahead, I see three paths distinct from one another and how the debris is stacked. One or all three could be dead ends. One could lead to the exit and one could lead to my death. One of these things is most definitely not like the other. A small smile forms on my face as I remember moments watching *Sesame Street* with Chase.

"Just like in college; when in doubt, pick *C*." I halfheartedly laugh at myself.

I choose the third path and take slow, deliberate steps. With all the debris of wood, paper, and other sundries, I have to protect my feet. I can't defend myself if I'm on the floor. I try to keep my eyes peeled in the darkness and focus on my surroundings. The cut on my forehead must have reopened, as blood taints my vision. I wipe my face with my busted hand and do nothing but smear the blood around. Getting to the end of the path, a pile of wood blocks me. Normally, I would turn around and retrace my steps. For some reason, I feel the need to push forward.

"Time to climb," I mumble to myself as I gauge the stability of the unsteady stack with my hands.

One step at a time, I move slowly up the hill. With my damaged hand, I touch what looks like a stable piece of wood only to have it shatter and force me to slide backwards. My right leg slips in between the slats of a pallet, and I wince as something gouges into my flesh. I looked down at my leg but can't see a thing. I struggle for stability and lean on my left side. Reaching down with my right hand, I push away the bits of splintered wood before feeling a metal nail embedded in my leg.

I continue feeling around, trying to ascertain which direction the nail is going in. If I knew it was bent, I could pull my leg out in the opposite direction. Taking a deep breath, I decide to pull my leg up and out between the two slats. The sound of the nail slowly exiting my skin is nauseating. With a slight popping sound, my leg is free and bleeding profusely. Looking back to the top of the pile, I realize that's my only destination. I go a little slower, more safely, and I manage to get there. I swing my legs to the other side of the pile and slowly make my way down. With each step, my right leg almost buckles. When I land on the floor, it completely gives way.

"Always had to be a contrarian, couldn't just double back . . ." Leave it to me to be my own worst enemy.

"Looks like you could use a hand." I look up to see Keith Garrison standing above me, his face etched with a sadistic smile, his thumbs through his belt loops and his hat perched on his head like always. "Looks like you've hurt yourself pretty bad there, detective. Doesn't make this game much fun when your hand's a mess and you can barely stand or run."

"I'm done playing," I say, gritting my teeth.

"This new attitude of yours wouldn't be due to that body upstairs, now would it?" he says with what sounds like happiness in his voice.

"You know it's not."

"Probably, but when an NYPD officer murders another officer, one has to question everything," he says with a full smile on his face.

"You know damn well he attacked m," I say, foolishly trying to defend my actions.

"Of course I do. But then again, no one really believes anything we say now. I mean a cop shows up to a crime scene and we're already blamed for it. We are racists, vile, evil, and all of us are being paid off. If you don't want to take responsibility for being a murderer, you can just blame the cop who arrested you. Society calls us pigs, spits on us, and does what they want. It's okay because the public and the liberal media allow it," he rants, completely off topic.

"Vent all you want. You're no better than a convicted felon."

"Never said I was." Garrison shrugs as if coming to terms with whom he is.

He reaches forward, grabs my shoulders, and lifts me up. With one swift move of my hand, his face changes and the smile is gone. He stumbles backwards, dropping me to the ground hard. He looks down at his stomach almost quizzically, the hilt of the small pocketknife sticking out of his skin. He grabs it, pulls it out, and throws it out of reach.

"That wasn't very nice. Not playing fair as one would expect from someone like you. You're no better than the rest of them either."

"You never play by the rules. Why should I?"

"Touché, pussycat." He pulls his gun out of its holster and aims it at me. As if by instinct, I raise my hands to block the shot, not like it'll do anything. He pulls the trigger, and I feel white-hot pain in my ankle, the sound of bone exploding on contact forcing a scream out of me that I've never heard before.

"You shouldn't have killed James. He was a good man even if he was a bit misguided. Followed the rules and did what I told him to like a good little soldier." He rubs the gun against his temple. I can't tell if he's fighting himself or trying to figure out where to shoot me next.

Rolling over on my stomach, I force myself to crawl past him. I can hear him laughing at how futile my escape attempt is. He fires again, and this time the burning pain is in my right thigh. Dropping my face onto the dirty floor, I feel blood leaving my body too fast for me to stay awake. I continue to drag myself away from him with my eyes closed and body weak.

"This is usually the part of the script where the villain tells the heroine all about their plan to take over the world. He tells her how he's going to get away with everything he's currently doing. Then, she goes on about how he won't get away with it. Rather counterproductive, don't you think? The funny thing is no matter what I say, it doesn't matter. Who really cares why I have done what I've done? You want the closure to make yourself feel better? Personally, I don't think it's important. I did what I did simply because I was told to do it. Is that enough for you? As you slowly slither away from me, you just have to accept that there's no reason for it. When you meet your maker, if in fact He exists, tell him I live my life to the best of my ability given the cards He dealt me."

I roll over on my back, finally accepting that I can't move any further. I hope Hadley's free. She'll be able to help Chase and Frankie through this. I guess this is karma. I wanted to die for so long, since I was in grammar school. This new fear, though, strangles the breath out of my chest. I don't want them to feel I gave up or be angry with me. I hope they'll find some peace about how this has to end.

Garrison's blurry silhouette walks closer to me, and I can tell I'm losing consciousness. The dirt from the floor has invaded all of my wounds and is caked to my skin. I swear I hear the metal garage door opening again, but I can't see anything. Garrison stands above me with his gun aimed and ready.

"Not how I wanted it to play out, but it ends today either way," he says, towering above me.

The metal clanging sound is louder, followed by various voices that I can't quite make out. The only thing I can hear is my own breathing. It's shallow and slow. I wonder if this is how Henry felt when he knew he was dying. The telltale click of the gun brings me back to attention. The sound of the gunshot ricochets around the building in my ears. The blurry silhouette stumbles backwards.

The voices are louder, screaming at one another. Another click and another bullet fires. The sound is followed by three quick explosive bursts. Garrison falls to the ground, unmoving. I grab my chest and feel the faintest wetness on my shirt. At first, I think it's my tears until the pain sets in. The red and blue lights flash from the doorway as I raise my hand to see it covered in blood. The agony and pressure in my chest are so great that I can't focus on anything else.

I think I see someone who looks like Hadley out of the corner of my eye. I believe Will checked Garrison's vitals before kneeling next to me. He's so close that I can make out his expression of fear mixed with anger. His two hands, fingers entwined, pressing down on me as he tries to stop the bleeding.

"You get him?" I sputter and bubble through the blood in my mouth.

"Through the chest," he says, his voice firm and unwavering. I wonder if he acted like this in the war zone—showing no emotion and just going on autopilot.

"Good job."

"Don't talk. Ambulance's here and they're getting the gurney," he says

"They say your life flashes before your eyes when you're about to die," I say to Will as my eyes try to focus on the ceiling.

"I heard something like that."

"My life must have sucked, because all I saw was my first boyfriend who was horrible at every sport he played." I try to laugh, but it causes too much pain. I force a smile with shallow breaths.

"Or you just remembered your biggest regret. You know, not dating women sooner?" I know Will's trying to keep me focused and aware.

"You think you're funny," I say as I hear the wheels of the gurney getting closer. I tug on Will's shirt, bringing his ear as close to my mouth as possible. "I killed James. He's upstairs. Tried to kill me. Lost control." I let him go, and he leans back on his heels. I can't tell if he's stunned, upset, or indifferent.

"You did what you had to do. Just like anyone of us would have done. You did good, boss," he says, finally letting go of my chest, and heads upstairs.

I hear the paramedics talking to one another as they stab me with needles and what I assume is an IV. My head rolls on the concrete beneath me, and I pray for the images of my loved ones to show, but they don't. I really hope there's a heaven willing to accept me.

"Pressures dropping, we've got a go now!" I hear one voice bark to the others. Next thing I know, I feel like I'm flying as they haul me away. I hear Will's voice and the sound of his military boots rushing toward us.

Looking to my left, I see Hadley sitting in the ambulance next to me. She's bandaged slightly, but it looks worse than it probably is. Will jumps in and sits next to her. He grabs my hand and holds tight. I hear the doors close as each breath weighs down my tired body. My eyes gaze back over to Hadley, but she won't look at me. I squeeze Will's hand hard as my breathing slows. I'm so very tired, and these men keep yelling at me to stay awake. But I can't.

Chapter Eleven

Many things can bring me out of a sound sleep. It could be sirens from the local precinct, someone honking their horn or revving their engine outside my window, or even just the birds chirping at an ungodly hour. Usually, it's the smell of a fresh pot of coffee. I remember my mother stood over me once and waved a fresh pot under my nose just to get me out of bed. I don't think it's the smell as much as it is the emotional attachment to the memories of my mother. That was our treat and reminder to touch base every once in a while. It was the only time I got to see her toward the end. This smell though—it's not coffee. It's something so much better and sweeter. Something I haven't had in years.

"Crêpes," I mumble as my stomach rumbles at the thought of the thin pancakes.

I open my eyes and take in the overly bright room. It's unfamiliar but feels like I've been here before. Part of me wonders if Frankie made pancakes, but she's a Bisquick kind of girl. These are originals, made from scratch. As I sit up, my right hand flies to my head, and I fall back to the bed. My chest hurts, my leg hurts, and frankly, the right side of my body feels like it's throbbing.

"Pinball machine migraine. What a way to start the day," I say, rubbing my eyes.

I slowly roll up to a sitting position and swing my feet to the floor. My left foot hits the fake lamb-like rug near the bed, and I wiggle my toes in its softness. My right foot hits with a loud thud. It's covered in a black metal or plastic boot. My fingers run along the edge of it, and I try to place why it's there. Forcing myself to stand up, the contraption on my right foot barely holds my weight, but it's good enough.

I lean on the wall by the door and notice my rainbow-colored hand. It doesn't hurt, but it feels off. There's a numbness in my pinky and ring fingers. If I could only remember why it's bruised and battered. I feel like I should be here, but yet I shouldn't.

"Jasmine Marie Steele, you better get your lazy butt out of bed and down to the breakfast table!" the softest voice with the hint of an accent yells from the kitchen. As if on pure muscle memory, I hobble out of the room and head downstairs.

I hear her singing in German as I take one step at a time, holding onto the railing. The hair on the back of my neck slowly rises to full attention. I haven't been in this foyer in years. The marble floor is shiny and clean, the crystal chandelier reflecting the light from the outside to beautiful prisms of color all over the walls. Everything is the same as it used to be—untouched by time or loss.

This place was my safe haven. I would plant flowers in the gardens, run errands to the bakery, or get cookies before going to the bank. All because my grandmother chose to spend time with me. I was allowed to be an adult like I wanted but also act the age that I was without fear of punishment or reprimanding. When everything in my world fell apart and my mother was lost in her own mind, I always found open arms waiting here for me.

"Your crêpes are getting cold! Don't make me come get you," she says with a hint of humor in her voice.

Stumbling into the kitchen, I see my grandmother gliding across the tile floor, placing food on my plate. Her pug, King, bounces around her feet, waiting for scraps of food to fall. She goes back to her singing, dancing while looking down at the four-legged friend by her side. The two of them move seamlessly around the kitchen, both appearing young, healthy, and unafraid of what the afterlife holds for them.

"King, you know I made some for you, but you have to wait until Mommy sits down." She places the pan back onto the stove and spins around. Her smile grows when she sees me. Her hair is perfectly done like I remember, her housecoat buttoned around her nightgown and her nails painted a bright red. If you asked her, she'd say she looked homely. To me, she never looked more beautiful.

"Morning, Oma." My voice surprises me at how stable it is.

"Jasmine, you are becoming such a beautiful woman," she says as her eyes scan my body.

"Complete with the newest fashion accessory of a boot. I hear it's all the rage at fashion week," I say, displaying my right foot like a model on *The Price is Right*.

"Yes, well, I said a beautiful woman. I never said anything about a coordinated one." She laughs to herself as she sits down in her chair. "Now sit before King eats your breakfast."

The slightly rotund pug sits in my chair, his tongue sticking out the right side along with a little of drool. I'm sure he's waiting for the go-ahead to devour my plate. When I push him gently, he hops to the floor and then up onto the chair next to my grandmother. She cuts a small piece of her pancake and holds it in her fingers. He turns his head slightly to the side and wraps his tongue around it, swallowing it whole.

"You made crêpes for me," I say as I sit staring at the meal in front of me.

"Of course I did. What kind of grandmother would I be if I forced you to eat your mother's pancakes? I love your mother, I do, but these are made with—"

"Lots of love, fresh stuff, and a sore back," I finish for her. It was one of her jokes. Everything from scratch was always made with someone in mind and the pain of standing there for hours. It's a lost art really; I can't cook for shit.

"See, you do listen," she says, smiling at me. King barks as if to let my grandmother know he wants more. "King, patience, my little one." She breaks off another small piece and feeds it to him.

A wave of pain jackhammers in my head, causing me to close my eyes and wince. The fork hits my plate harder than I'd like, and I forced myself to swallow what's in my mouth. I feel her hand rubbing my forearm. She used to do that to calm me down.

"Are you okay, honey?" she asks softly.

"Just a headache," I say as the pain fades. I take another bite, and a slight moan emanates from me. "These are so good, Grandma. Hits the spot. It feels like forever since I've had your cooking."

"Well, some people are worth slaving over a counter for. Oh gosh, I almost forgot!" She hops up from her chair and heads back into the kitchen.

King leans forward, his front paws on the table, and grabs what's left of the cut crepe in his mouth. He sounds like he's saying yum as he chews. If I didn't know any better, I'd say he was smiling at me when he was done. A slamming pain in my chest stops my train of thought, and I grab the chair for support.

"Jasmine, are you sure you're okay?" I feel her hand rubbing up and down my back to comfort me.

"Yeah, it'll pass," I say as she pours me a cup of coffee. She pours herself one as well before resting the pot on a folded washcloth in the center of the table.

"You should have that checked out. You might not listen to your mother, but you always listen to this old lady who loves you. Please go see a doctor. I don't like these chest pains you keep getting. Maybe go see Opa's doctor; he swears by him. Then again maybe not. He is dead after all," she says with a slight chuckle.

"You know I was born with them, Grandma. They come and go. I promise I'm taking good care of myself, so there's no need to worry," I say, taking a sip of my coffee.

"This coming from the woman with that contraption on her foot and a multicolored hand?" I watch as she turns toward King and feeds him the rest of her breakfast. "I know you're gay; you don't need to have a rainbow hand to prove it." She giggles at her own joke.

She turns back to face me, and she's aged considerably, her hair no longer perfectly coiffed upon her head and her eyes sullener than before. Her back is curved ever so slightly and her shoulders hunched inward, her powerful stance weakened by an aging body.

"You're not eating?" I ask, trying to catch the emotion in my throat before she can hear it.

"You know between my teeth and my stomach I can't eat much. Too much pain, Jasmine." She turns to the empty chair next to her and her eyes glaze over with unshed tears. "My King would've helped me. He always made me feel better. I promised him we'd go together, Jasmine. You make sure he's with me, okay?" She places her hand over mine as it violently shakes.

"Oma, why don't you let me call your doctor. I'll take you to your appointment and maybe we can see what's going on." I say, placing my left hand over hers resting on my right.

"Oh, Jasmine, those crooks only tell you you're old and to go home. They give you some pill to take that just makes you feel worse, but it makes them money. I'm old, sweetheart. This is what happens," she says as a few tears break free and roll down her face.

"There has to be something you can take for your pain." I gag as a piercing hot bolt of pain radiates through my chest. My grandmother watches and squeezes my hand tightly. After a few deep breaths, the pain subsides.

"Nothing works for me now, Jasmine. I have so many pills and none of them do anything for me. Your mother sets them out by date and time, but they don't help. No, I'm tired of pills. No, you eat up," she says with a halfhearted smile as the tears continue.

I take a few more bites of the food on my plate and wash it down with more coffee. She watches me, and I swear I can see more wrinkles forming with each minute that passes by.

"You're just like your mother," she says, taking me off guard.

"How so?" I place my fork down beside my empty plate.

"For one, you both love salt. Gosh, your mother could bury a small country under a pile of that stuff. You're both also so stubborn about how you do things. Can't see a tree for the damn forest. You have so much in front of you, but you always look behind you. Tell me, how does your ass look?"

"I don't know, bigger than I'd like," I say, dismissing her seriousness and putting a little levity in the conversation.

"Exactly. You're so focused on what's in the past that you can't even see the road ahead. Jasmine, you and I didn't see eye to eye on everything, but you could always talk to me. What aren't you telling me?"

"There's nothing to talk about, Oma."

She removes her hand from mine and taps it gently. She leans back in her chair and simply nods her head. Her eyes see right through me, and I know she's waiting for me to talk. This isn't real; it can't be.

"Chase is going to have a lot of questions. He's going to be very scared like we all are. He'll also be very attached to you for some time."

"Of course. He lost his parents."

"You died on him too," she says calmly.

"No, I didn't." If this is all in my head, I'm not dead. The last thing I remember is being in an ambulance and heading to the hospital. If anyone can save my life, I assume it's the doctors there.

"You coded on the way. Captain Udall was driving Chase and Frankie to the hospital when the call went out over the radio. Your boss is not the bad guy you think he is. All of this stuff going on is much bigger than him," she says, her tone shifting to an authoritative one. "Frankie's holding it together as best she can for Chase. You made a good choice in leaving him to her in a worst-case scenario." She answers my unspoken question.

"Oma, I love you, but none of this makes sense. If it's bigger than the captain—" My words are cut short by my heart racing and a shot of electricity through the cavity.

"Probably trying to remove the bullet from your chest without hitting any major arteries. They could also be repairing the damage it caused. I couldn't tell you which one it is though."

"I'll do what I have to do, just like I've always done. Just like you and Mom raised me to do," I say, trying to get my breathing under control.

"I'm not questioning your judgment, but you are."

"Maybe I shouldn't have gone alone. Maybe I should've called for help. There are so many different ways this could have gone. Everyone's going to question what I did, why I did it, and Lord knows I'll be reprimanded. But who could I trust?"

"All of those questions have many different answers. Hadley might have died regardless of whether you showed up or not. James might've taken the call, and you don't know how that would have ended either."

"I should have leaned on my partner more and asked for his help."

"Well, he found you and killed Garrison. You can't try to figure it all out, Jasmine. Life is a game of chess, and everyone has their part to play. Whatever decisions or moves you've made, they're done. Stop trying to analyze or rationalize it all. It'll just give you a worse headache," she says in a soothing voice.

"I killed James. I murdered him."

"Yes, you did. I'm sure you feel guilt like you've never felt before. You chose to remove another person from this planet, but he was going to do the same to you. There are some people in this world that don't deserve to live because of the choices they've made. You decided Hadley's life and your life were not his to dispose of. There is no guilt or shame in that."

"I'm no better than him, Oma."

"How can you be so sure about that? He would have killed the two of you without a second thought. He offered Hadley freedom, and she still denied him. That man lost his way. He was the immovable object, and you are the unstoppable force. One of you had to move."

"Maybe, but Garrison—"

"Jasmine, stop it. He was working a job for his father. Your only concern was to find the connection, the paper trail if you will. That information was to be used to bring the man and his powerful lackeys to justice. Nothing more, nothing less."

"There isn't going to be any justice. There was no evidence; I found out about everything because of his stupidity. How will justice be served when there's nothing to present?" I say exasperatedly.

"Maybe not now, but people like him never stay hidden for long. Keith Garrison was killed at the hands of the NYPD. His father won't go into hiding. You just have to wait, watch, and catch them when the time is right."

"And if I fail?" I ask, my voice sheepish and small.

"Then you fail. The world still goes on and crime will continue. The man who killed your brother and sister-in-law is dead. He can't hurt you anymore, and he can't haunt your dreams. If nothing else, you have closure. Let him go."

"There's more to the case than just that one man," I say, defending myself.

"That's true. Let me ask you something, though. What can you do if you're dead?"

"Anything is better than just sitting on the sidelines."

"You need to let this go. Chase and Frankie need you to move on. Don't bury yourself in the past like you always do. Don't allow this case to hinder your ability to enjoy life. Go out and live. Be different from your mother and I. Live your life for you instead of some obligation to your family. You've given us so many years of your life. Why not keep the rest for yourself? Give Chase the experiences you want to share with him. Let him be a boy and see his superhero as someone who never goes back on her word," she pleads with me.

"I've never broken my promises to him and I never will. Not if I can help it," I say a little harsher than I meant to.

"Yet here you are," she answers with the same tone to me. "My mother always told me it doesn't matter what I do, my children will be who they were meant to be. Chase is going to interpret everything you've said or done in his own way. He's growing up, learning about the world, and processing it in a way we can't understand. He saw you die, Jasmine. That's black-and-white to him. You abandoned him."

My grandmother grabs the dishes from the table and heads to the kitchen. She walks to the sink and turns the water on. It is routine. The house was always immaculate, even when she could barely sweep the floor. She took pride in her home, and it's a trait I wish I had. It was part of the reason I couldn't live here when she died. I could never take care of it the same way she did.

"You need to figure out your own way, now. You can't go on living in the past and let it run you around like a dog on a leash. You have to let us all go."

"I don't understand," I say, the emotion in my voice betraying my stoic face.

She turns and leans back against the counter. Her skin tone is ashen and her bones protrude everywhere. Her spine has curved so severely she can barely look up at me, her eyes hidden by the excess skin of her eyelids, her wedding ring loose on her finger. Her toothless smile is weak and shallow. This was what she looked like when I last saw her. When she last opened her eyes and told me she loved me.

"Jasmine, there is a time and place to remember us. When you have a cup of coffee or tea, think of your mother. When at a baseball game, think of your brother. When someone talks in circles when you just want them to get to the point, think of your father." She laughs at the last line before coughing violently. It takes a few moments for her to stop. "When your garden of lilies blooms in the spring, think of me. You were there for all of us when we needed you most. We're not afraid anymore. Go be there for yourself, Chase, and Frankie."

"I have reasons for holding onto the past, Oma. It's not something I can just walk away from," I say as tears falls uninhibited down my cheeks.

"You've never had a valid reason. You knew what to do when we needed you. You never faced your emotions because you had something to focus on. Now you don't have us to worry about or to guide you. Right now, you're just like I was right before I passed on. You're afraid, and you're letting it paralyze you."

"Oma, I have a gun. Bad guys are afraid of me, not the other way around," I say, trying to change the conversation. The constant burning in my chest grows, but my emotions rage wildly.

"In all my years, I never thought I would be sitting here trying to explain the meaning of life to you," she says, and she shakes her head.

"I don't need you to explain it, Oma. You live. If you're lucky, you get to pass along your feelings, emotions, and lessons to someone else. Then you die. It's truly as simple as that," I say, trying to end the conversation as I rub my chest to calm the burning.

"Your father never understood either. Your mother, sometimes she got it. Other times I swear she would forget her ass if it wasn't attached.

Don't get me started on your brother. He was too smart for his own good."

It always made me smile when my grandmother would curse. She used to do it in German, thinking we'd never know. Henry and I used to run around the house screaming *scheisse,* thinking we were being funny. It wasn't until Mom slapped us both and Oma laughed hysterically that we realized it was a curse word. It's those memories that remind me of her classic beauty and humor. There were things said at the end that should never have been said. I personally blame age, as it makes it harder to express one's emotions since your mind is not as sharp as it used to be.

"I'm not much better than Henry." I smile.

"You're not your brother. You never were. Jasmine, your grandfather and I saved our whole lives so we could leave our children a little something. You sacrifice the peaceful hours while your child is sleeping in order to work on creating a business. They go to the park or have sleepovers with friends and you are making phone calls to drum up interest and a client list. You miss things as they grow up, and sometimes you make decisions you'll never forgive yourself for. We might have looked like we were always working, but our kids never went without. We always had a family dinner. They both had clothing, a roof over their head, and schooling. When they were older, your grandfather and I traveled and learned about the world. Our lives weren't perfect, but we lived the best way we knew how."

She shuffles her sock covered feet over to me. She staggers a bit, her balance giving her trouble. Her hands shake violently and her eyes are cast downward. I jump up to meet her halfway. She reaches up and grasps the sides of my face. Her body is an obvious shrunken and defiant shell of what she used to be. Her thumbs graze my cheekbones, and I looked down at her realizing, her height has shrunk along with her lifespan.

"You have everything you need to make decisions—and good ones at that. You have to do what your mother and I had to do when we raised our children. You have to trust yourself," she says as her German accent almost overwhelms each word.

"I don't want to die." The words out of my mouth are barely above a whisper.

"Then don't," she replies simply.

She wipes away my tears with her thumbs as the water flows unimpeded from her eyes. She pulls my head down and kisses my forehead. A wave of pain so strong constricts in my chest, forcing me to my knees. My entire body feels like it's on fire after being electrocuted. My hands go to my chest and squeeze at the skin. Oma pulls my head to her chest and wraps her arms around my shoulders. She begins to hum a song from my childhood. Instantly, it calms me.

"What's going to happen to me?" I say, still gasping for air.

"I don't know, sweetheart. You closed your eyes."

"I just wanted to rest."

"My love, living people keep their eyes open and alert. They choose to stay awake instead of running and hiding in the darkness. Dying people close their eyes for a little rest," she says soothingly.

"So, I'm dying," I conclude matter-of-factly.

"It seems to me like that's up to you," she says as another shot of pain causes me to dig my nails into my own skin.

"Oma, tell me what to do. Please," I almost beg.

"I can't. You say you don't want to die, but your actions prove you don't want to live either. You have to choose."

"But if I choose"—I look up, meeting my grandmother's gaze—"you go away."

"Oh, my dear Jasmine, I'm already gone."

It's those words that hit me harder than anything in the outside world. No matter how much I want to hold them again or tell them I love you one more time, I can't. It doesn't quite seem fair, but I'm sure everyone experiences this.

"What happens when I've made a choice?"

"That's truly up to you. Just know that we all love you very much and we live on in you and Chase," she says, pulling me into the tightest hug I have felt in a very long time.

The smell of her perfume fills my nostrils, and I swear I can hear her heart beating in my ears. As the pain increases and I feel my body going limp, she sings a German lullaby to me. Together, we end up on the cool tile floor and she rocks me back and forth. As the darkness overwhelms me, her voice fades, no matter how much I try to keep hold of it.

Chapter Twelve

The agonizing pain and burning in my chest slowly ends as an odd peacefulness washes over me. I hear someone humming the lullaby my Oma was singing to me. The voice is different but soft and comforting. As my consciousness comes back to me, every nerve in my body flares. The intense pain is agonizing, mind-numbing, and overwhelming. I feel someone's hand grasp mine, but I can't squeeze theirs in return. It's as if the muscles don't want to listen and do what they're told.

My entire body feels stiff and foreign. Trying to move feels like wading through quicksand while wearing cement shoes. I can hear more voices, indiscriminate sounds in what I assume is conversation. Trying to decipher it is difficult. The humming is so close to my ear that it's crystal clear. My hand being squeezed, my forearm being rubbed, and the voice grab my focus.

My muscles finally wake up and my right leg twitches in response. The movement is subtle, and it feels confined, similar to the boot in my dream. It's then that the memory of the bullet shattering my ankle flashes in my mind. My breathing quickens, and I feel my fingers move. My right hand is locked in place; it must be a full cast of some kind.

The pain seeps throughout my body, and I can hear the beeping of my heart rate increasing in speed. The hand holding mine abruptly let's go. The voices above me get louder, and the comforting melodic noise on my left gets further away. Using all the energy I can muster, my left arm spastically flails out in the direction of the humming sound.

I try to talk but there's something obstructing me, probably a tube in my throat. I fight to mouth anything or whisper, but I can't. I try to force my eyes open, but they feel so heavy and unmoving. I reach out again, a little more in control, and come in contact with a solid form. A smaller hand grabs mine, and the humming stops. The bed dips slightly, and I feel a weight rest on my shoulder.

"Aunt Jasmine, wake up for me, okay? Please don't go away," Chase says barely above a whisper.

I hear his emotions radiating through his words. I force my left eyelid open just a sliver. The brightness virtually blinds me, and I twitch to try to make it go away. Slowly, shapes come into view and my gaze rests on a mat of hair in front of my face. Scanning lower on my body, I see a hint of his black cast. Somehow, he managed to worm his way onto the bed while the doctors were working on me.

"Detective Steele, can you hear me?" the doctor on my right says a little louder than necessary.

I can't reply verbally, so I slightly nod in response.

"That's good. Do you know where you are?"

My gaze darts across the room. Seeing all the machines and feeling the needles in my arm, I must be at the hospital, and the sheer number of them leads me to believe I'm in the intensive care unit. Once again, I nod in response.

"Good, good. You have a breathing tube in your throat. We can remove it, but it's going to hurt. If you struggle to breathe on your own, we're going to have to put it back in. Do you understand?" the doctor asks, and I reply in the same fashion as before. "All right, I'm going to need you to take a deep breath."

The doctor leans over my body, and I can feel Chase trying to disentangle himself from me.

"You're fine, honey, don't move," the doctor says, placing his hand on Chase's lower back. "All right, detective, take a deep breath in."

I do what I'm told and intake as much air as possible. The doctor pulls on the tube, and I feel it ripping up my throat like a wrecking ball to a building. It's painful, but a welcomed discomfort. The minute it exits my mouth, I break into a coughing fit, each spasm causing a strain on my surgically repaired chest. I feel Chase wrap his arms around my stomach, trying to comfort me. I see Frankie to my left, smiling. She must have been the source of the humming, and I'm not surprised. The doctor mumbles something to her. She nods in reply, and he leaves us alone.

"How are you feeling?" the lump on the bed asks me.

"Like someone punched me in the chest a few hundred times," I manage to eke out, my voice still very scratchy.

"Uncle Victor said they had to open your chest. He told me to be very careful when I hug you. Touch the belly, not the chest." His little arms tighten around my waist as he puts all of his love into a hug. It hurts a little, but it's well worth it. I rub his back with my left arm. "You died," he weakly says to the side of my chest.

"I came back. Nothing could keep me away from you," I say, trying to reassure him.

"Promise me you won't do that again. Aunt Frankie, she was really upset at you. Girls cry a lot," he says innocently.

I stifle my laughter at his comments. I hold his left hand with my cast hand as much as I physically can. Looking to the right side of my bed, I see Victor and Hadley, her arm in a sling, a bruised cheek, and her eyes red and puffy. Our resident medical examiner looks the worse for wear, his face firm in a stoic expression. I've seen that look before. He tries to hide his emotions and goes into professional mode. It's hard to break him out of it.

"Hey, Chase, why don't you go downstairs and get some ice cream? Your daddy once told me that it helped heal anything wrong with you. That way the doctors can tell your auntie what happened." He looks up from my shoulder and studies me. I smile at him, nod, and run the fingers of my left hand through his hair.

"Promise me you won't go anywhere!" he says, sounding just like his father.

"I promise. Just make sure you bring some back for me."

Chase kisses me on the cheek before carefully sliding off the bed. Hadley places her hand on my shoulder and squeezes it gently. Victor says nothing as he watches the two of them leave. He walks up to the side of my bed, his facial expression never changing.

"Give it to me straight, doc."

Victor looks at Frankie as if waiting for permission to tell me. His hand runs through his messy hair, he swallows hard, and I can tell he's delaying the inevitable.

"Okay, you were shot in the ankle. Doctors rebuilt it with various metal and donor bones. Should be able to walk like normal in time. Your hand required a different surgery to fix it. Again, you should be fine with some physical therapy. Yet another bullet in the thigh, but it missed all the major arteries and lodged in the muscle. After it was removed, doctors closed it up with no problems. You following me so far?" he says, sounding like my high school biology teacher.

"Yeah. Before you get to the good stuff, how'd you find me?" I ask, trying to postpone the explanation of my chest wound.

"Frankie woke up and realized you weren't in bed. Hadley never returned from the film shoot, so we got concerned. Will tried to call James a couple of times, but he never answered. Captain asked our tech team to track your phone. Once we realized you were at the film shoot, Will and the other officers went over there immediately . . ." Victor trails off.

"In route, Will called for backup and an ambulance to meet us there. Apparently, Will found Hadley cowering in a corner outside of the warehouse. She told him what happened, and he went in there like any Marine would," Frankie said, adding her voice to the mix.

"Thank you," I say, measuring my voice carefully. "Basically, after all this, I've got a biotic zombie ankle and fat saved my life by slowing down the bullet in my thigh." I smile, trying to lighten the mood before it gets very serious.

Neither one of them see the humor in any of my words. I feel Frankie slide her hand in mine and squeeze. Victor clears his throat and waits for me to stop being childish.

"You have minor lacerations to your forehead. It took only a few stitches to close up, and it shouldn't scar." He pauses, rubs the back of his neck, and for the first time I see how truly tired he is. "Garrison shot you in the chest at almost point-blank range. Will shot him almost simultaneously, forcing Garrison to lose his balance. That pretty much saved your life. The bullet nicked your heart, and considering your heart murmur, it was bad. You wouldn't stop bleeding. You coded once in the ambulance, once in the trauma room, and one more time on the table. The last one was the longest. One doctor said to call it, but you came back. Heart's been fixed, but the strain on it has yet to be determined. No matter what, it's going to take you months to get back up and running at a hundred percent," Victor finishes.

"Yet to be determined?" I ask, concerned.

"Jasmine, your heart stopped three times. You have no idea the amount of work it takes to bring you back and what that does to the human body. I have no clue as to what future issues could or might be. You might not face any issues, if you're blessed. All I can tell you is your lifestyle has to change, and you better start taking care of yourself," he says, sounding more like a parent than a close friend, but I assume he thinks I need that right now. I don't know what I need.

"I know this is a lot to take in. I know you don't want to hear it, but Will blames himself for you being shot. That silly Marine thinks if he shot half a second earlier or at a different angle, he would have missed you," Frankie says softly next to me.

"He did everything he could," I say solemnly as I look between the two of them. Neither one meets my gaze. "You both told him that, right?"

"We were a little busy trying to keep you alive, among other things," Victor says, sounding angrier by the second.

"Victor, why don't you get the others and head back to the safe house. Eat her ice cream and get some rest. I'll call you if anything changes." Frankie smiles at Victor, and he storms out of the room.

"I think he needs a nap," I say in jest.

"I think sleep has been rather elusive for all of us," Frankie says as she stares at our entwined hands. She looks truly exhausted. Her hair is a mess, her eyes highlighted by dark circles under them, her skin tone drawn and ashen. I don't know how long I've been out, but it's obviously taken a toll.

"Maybe you should go home too. Some sleep would do you good. I'll be fine now. I'm awake," I say to Frankie, but she doesn't acknowledge me. Her focus remains solely on our hands.

"When they brought you in, no one would tell me anything. I could hear Hadley screaming from the other end of the hall. She was hysterically crying, calling out your name and frantically reaching for you. I stood in the hallway as your bloody body was rolled past on a gurney. I vaguely heard the paramedics rattle off some numbers, things I was trained to look for but that didn't seem to matter right then. I just kept wondering how so much blood could come from one person. Someone was sitting on top of you doing CPR and then you disappeared into an elevator. I couldn't hold your hand or touch you and tell you I love you. Nothing. One minute you were in my arms sleeping, in the next you were dying in front of me," she says, her voice small and withdrawn.

"I'm sure the doctors were doing everything they could. You shouldn't have seen that. I'm so sorry you did," I say, trying to calm her.

"Do you know Victor followed them all the way up to the OR? They were yelling at him about protocol, procedures, and some other crap, but he didn't care. Our medical examiner jumped in when he heard someone asking for help. Our friend who deals with death, destruction in the end of life, made sure you lived. Even when they wanted to call it, he begged for more time. His hands were in your chest, squeezing your heart while he begged for patience. He's not mad or just needs a nap . . . he's emotionally drained and tired, Jasmine. He stepped in where I couldn't, and for that I will be forever grateful." Her voice cracks and a single tear rolls down her face.

I wish I could say something to comfort her, but no words come to mind. While all this was going on, I was having pancakes with my Oma, unconscious. I don't know what to do with this information she's given me.

"I'm so sorry." It sounds like such a weak comment coming out of my mouth. She looks up at me, and her expression tells me my words have fallen short.

"Sorry?" she says, her voice firmer than before. "I wish I knew how to respond to that, Jasmine. I want to be rational and tell you that you have nothing to be sorry about. Part of me wants to just wrap my arms around you and tell you everything is perfectly fine. I want to be an adult and rise above this, but inside I want to say some really not nice things."

"So, say them. I think you've earned that right," I say.

"You left in the middle of the night without telling anyone. You knew the dangers and the risk you were taking, but you never thought to wake me the fuck up? You never said goodbye. You never gave any of us the respect of at least leaving a note to tell us where you were going. No, you just ran off and left the rest of us behind. Are you truly that stupid? After all your education, I had assumed you learned something. I must've been wrong, because why the fuck did you think it's okay to put yourself in such extreme danger when you have a family at home? Do we mean that little to you?" Her face is red and tears flow freely down her cheeks. I can feel all the fear oozing out of her pores as her words cut into my battered skin.

"Frankie . . ." I try to say something, but she holds her hand up stopping me.

"It's not just about you anymore, Jasmine! You didn't think twice about leaving Chase behind. You're his fucking mother, Jasmine!" I open my mouth to protest, but once again she shuts me up. "I don't care that you didn't give birth to him. He called you his other mother when he begged the doctor to save your life. He cried his eyes out for three nights while you were asleep asking God why he hated him so much. He cried on my shoulder, asking me why everyone he loved ends up dying." She spits a bit of her tears at me as they continue the feverish trail down her face. Her mind so focused on venting, she does nothing to wipe them away.

"I know what I did was stupid."

"Nobody knew what your plans were, so I had to call up your lawyer and have him come down here. Cary came rushing over with your power of attorney paperwork and a will I didn't know you had. He tells me one of your wishes was to give me guardianship of Chase. Not only was I still your medical proxy, but now I had someone asking me if I would take your nephew if you died."

"I made that will a long time ago. I never expected it to see the light of day," I say, trying to defend the only actions that I could.

"They asked me if you wanted to be on life support or if that was a thing you despised. I was asked what your end-of-life choices were. Did you have a plot or did you want to be cremated? I had no idea." Her voice shatters as she struggles to verbalize everything I put her through. "They asked me things . . . things I never thought I'd have to answer, let alone have the right to. I signed papers, Jasmine. Legal fucking papers. Did you know they have a judge here for just these reasons? Upstairs, in the criminal ward, they have a judge. He approved all the paperwork that you had ready and waiting with your will. I signed them."

She lets go of my hand, stands up, and begins pacing the floor. Realization sinks in as to what papers she's referring to. If I was ever incapacitated, I had legal documents drawn up so Frankie would be able to adopt Chase as soon as humanly possible. Cary knew that after my brother's passing, this was something I wanted done before my body was cold. It would make me feel better, even if I wasn't aware of it, that Chase was adopted and safe before I passed away.

"I'm sorry. I don't know how many times I can say that. I also know you didn't have to sign those papers," I say sheepishly.

She turns her head sharply to face me, her eyes showcasing pure anger piercing through the tears. She walks back to the side of the bed and places her left hand next to mine for balance.

"Of course I did, Jasmine. I always wanted to, but you never asked me. He was always ours, regardless of how he came to be there. But it ends now. You can't just go off half-cocked anymore. You lost that right to just leave us like that. You understand me?" she says, trying to calm herself down.

I take her hand in mine and lift it to my lips. I so missed those moments when I could just wrap my arms around her and make the world disappear. No matter how far apart we seem to get, our hearts are like magnets constantly pulling us back to one another.

"So, where do we go from here? Is Chase staying with you?"

"I had Cary get his associate to put my apartment on the market. Before you say anything, it's too far away and the mortgage is a lot of money. I don't want to remove Chase from the school he's already attending, and you know my place does not have enough bedrooms. Your house is missing, but the insurance has paid enough, and Will has been watching the rebuild. It helps to have several volunteers in all aspects of construction getting it done quickly. Last I checked, the framing was done and they were putting the outside walls up. Until it's complete, we're renting a three-bedroom apartment. Chase has his room, you have yours, and I will have my own."

"We don't need to spend that much money on a three-bedroom apartment. We could—"

"No, we can't. This isn't going to be a get back together, move in, and go right back to where we were before. We've both grown up and changed over our time apart. You're seriously injured and have a long recovery ahead of you. Not only do we have to learn to live together again, we have to learn to coparent. You don't get to shut me out this time, Jasmine. Legally, the boy is both of ours."

"As long as I have some video games during my recovery, I'll be good," I say nonchalantly. I can tell by her expression that she realizes I've accepted her terms and conditions.

"They're in the living room until the house is finished. Then I expect your games to be in the basement. I don't want to hear gunfire at four o'clock in the morning." Her cell phone begins to ring, and she answers it on speaker phone.

"Chase refused to lie down before he spoke to you again, okay?" Hadley says, her voice very tired.

"Sure, no problem. You're on speaker," Frankie says in response.

"Auntie Jazz, I forgot to tell you Aunt Frankie moved in with us. Some guy in a suit told me she gets to be my mommy too. Isn't that awesome?" I hear him yawn after he finishes speaking.

"She told me all about it, buddy. I hope you're okay with it."

"Why not? Do you not want her to be? I think she's cool. She bought us a new Xbox and PlayStation to replace the ones damaged in the fire. Plus, she gives really good hugs for a girl," he finishes through another yawn. "I'm going to go to bed now, night."

"Night, kiddo," Frankie says before I can.

The phone line goes dead just as there's knocking on the door. Captain Udall stands in the doorway. Frankie stands up, kisses my forehead, and exits the room, leaving the two of us alone.

"Checking in on me?" I say lightheartedly to my boss.

"I'm actually on my way out. I have a meeting with IAB and a shit ton of paperwork to do back at the office. I heard you were awake, and I wanted to see it for myself," he says, but I can tell there's more.

"Don't worry, boss. I'll be back good as new."

"You will take as much time as necessary to fully heal. When you get back, you'll be sitting behind a desk until you pass all of your psychological and physical evaluations. You're one of the very best, so that's an order. If I hear you're not listening to your doctors or Frankie, I'll come after you myself."

"I'll do it, but I won't like it."

"I know that. I also want you to know that you're no longer on the Garrison case. We have a team of people looking into it and seeing how far up it goes. Keith might have slipped under our noses and infiltrated our ranks, but he got orders from his father and other people. Either way, it's out of your hands."

"Captain—"

"Feel better, Jasmine," he says, cutting me off before exiting my room.

Silence fills the air and overwhelms me. Reaching over to the IV drip, I push the button for more pain medication. With all of the information bouncing around in my head, the nothingness of sleep allows for a few hours of peace. When I wake up, I can face everything then.

Chapter Thirteen

It's been about fourteen months of painful physical therapy, psychiatrist visits, and a lot of boring alone time at home. Not being allowed in the office to do anything really puts me in a sour mood. I want to get back to work, even if it's at my desk to push papers. I need to feel useful.

It's led to some fights and uncomfortable conversations with Frankie. I guess that's to be expected with her legally having a say over Chase now. It was the right thing to do, but sometimes my foot goes right into my mouth about it. We have to compromise and adjust. I'm really going out of my mind here with nothing to do.

Chase has been doing much better. We've been working on a schedule for all of his interests. Baseball, lacrosse, and basketball are all in the same spring to summer months, and we struggle to make it work. Luckily, I can drive him around and enjoy watching him play. I'm sure Henry would have loved this. Maybe Chase is right, maybe they can see him living life. Hopefully, my brother is proud of us. We're not perfect, but we are trying to live the best way we can.

Eventually, Chase is going to have to knock down some of his activities. Between classes, chores around the house, and his video games, there will only be time for one other thing. Right now, I can say with the utmost certainty he's just enjoying every day. He reminds me a lot of myself when I was his age. We both can pick up any sport and just do it with varying degrees of success. Even at my old age, I am still involved in some sport or another. Right now, I'd say it's more track as I run after assholes who run away from me.

Frankie and I have been doing much better in these fourteen months. We've learned to communicate more, which has come out of therapy, truthfully. I need to learn to open up more and tell her what I'm feeling. She moved into our old bedroom about a month ago, and with the exception of her snoring, it's good. She turned the old room into an office. She likes to work from home if she can. It's a nice change.

Water splashes my face, and I laugh as Chase jumps in the pool and swims after Frankie. They're my life, and they make me happier than I've ever been. Looking around the pool, seeing my friends and family, makes me realize how I've been blessed. On top of that, I have a partner that I like for once. Tyler made Will my partner in crime at my request. Granted, we are still taking it slow due to my semi-desk duty, but Will is okay with that. We'll get back out there when the doc and my body say it's all clear. I'm almost there.

Standing up, I walk inside the house and down the stairs to the basement. Opening the door to my game room, I close it behind me. Flipping on the switch, I illuminate the photo-and information-covered walls. Each image has listed information underneath it, string tracing one peg to another. No matter how amazing my life might be upstairs, down here it's a painful reminder of the one who got away. Call it an obsession. Call it whatever you like. I know eventually he'll make a mistake, and I'll be there to catch him.

Sitting down in my chair, I look at photos from the latest crime scene. My mother's voice echoes in my head: "A woman's work is never done."

THE END

About Author

Kimberly Amato is the author of the Jasmine Steele Mystery Series and Enemy. Having won awards for a TV Pilot she co-wrote & produced, she dove headfirst into writing novels. Always creating, jotting down new ideas & unafraid to try new genres, Kimberly writes mysteries, crime, romance, sci-fi & more. Beyond that, she's a podcaster with her wife, Sheila, for the show Forever Fangirls reviewing TV and film on streaming services and in theaters. Kimberly enjoys keeping in touch with her readers. You can find her by using the links below or going to her website KimberlyAmato.com.

amazon.com/stores/Kimberly-Amato/author/B00RKJDIXA

bookbub.com/authors/kimberly-amato

facebook.com/thekimberlyamato

instagram.com/kimberlyamato

Go to the link below to stay up to date on new releases and more!
https://www.kimberlyamato.com/newsletter

Also By Kimberly Amato

THE STEELE SERIES

Steele Intent (Book 1)

Melting Steele (Book 2)

Breaking Steele (Book 3)

Cold Steele (Book 4)

Steele Shield (Book 5)

Steele Influence (Book 6)

STANDALONES

Enemy

www.ingramcontent.com/pod-product-compliance
Lightning Source LLC
Chambersburg PA
CBHW031320160726
47993CB00001B/487